In Plain Sight

In Plain Sight

By:

Michelle Sutton

Desert Breeze Publishing, Inc.
24303 Walnut St, Ste C
Newhall, CA 91321

http://www.DesertBreezePublishing.com

Copyright © 2010 by Michelle Sutton
ISBN 10: 1-61252- 873-2
ISBN 13: 978-1-61252-873-1

Published in the United States of America
Electronic Publish Date: April 1, 2010
Print Publish Date: July 2013

Editor-In-Chief: Gail R. Delaney
Content Editor: Gail R. Delaney
Marketing Director: Jenifer Ranieri
Cover Artist: Jenifer Ranieri

Cover Art Copyright by Desert Breeze Publishing, Inc © 2010

Dedication and Acknowledgement

I would like to dedicate this story to women who have at one time or another been duped by a man into thinking that he truly cared, when in reality it was a deception from the moment you first met.

To the staff at Desert Breeze Publishing for their encouragement and support. Thank you! A special thank you goes to Editor-in-Chief, Gail Delaney, for loving my first story enough to agree to a second installment with the same characters. I wanted to write a novel about Bojan's sister, Jovana, and share her story with readers. You've given me the opportunity to do just that. Thanks also to my author bud Deb Ullrick for her ongoing encouragement and to Kim Byrd for being excited about this project and for reading my rough drafts.

Last, I want to thank God for inspiring me to write true-to-life stories that challenge people to look into their hearts and do an honest assessment of themselves and their motivations for everything they do... especially when it comes to romantic relationships. I also want to thank my family and my writer friends for their continuing support. God bless you all.

Prologue

The moment Kurt Smith sat down and peered into her intense brown eyes he knew she was the one. Five years of searching had brought him to her table. Yes, fate had chosen this petite woman to replace his wife. She wasn't as attractive as his Mary had been, but this woman looked so much like her they could have been sisters. The urge to reach out and stroke her cheek made his fingers twitch, but he held back. Now was not the time. That would come later, once he'd won her trust and her heart.

Her face flushed red and she cleared her throat. She'd caught him staring at her.

She asked him in heavily accented English, "May I take order for you, sir?"

Scanning her from head to toe, he nodded his appreciation. This adventure would be sweet. He was sure of it. His beloved Mary had never listened to reason, but he had a feeling this woman would do whatever he asked. As he searched her eyes he sensed some weakness from her past, like she'd tried to please a man before and failed. The hint of distrust in her eyes told him she'd paid for her mistakes. He would teach her how to please a man and succeed this time.

Smiling softly, he answered her request and pointed at the menu. "Yes, I'd like the number one special. The short stack with two eggs over easy and hash browns on the side."

He saw her glance at his ring finger as she wrote his order on the tablet she carried.

She was fighting her attraction to him. He sensed that as strongly as he could smell the bacon cooking on the grill. He would accommodate her desires, but not in a way that she would expect. No, he'd be patient and slowly win her over until she begged him to meet her womanly needs. He was a bit older than her, but up until now that had worked to his advantage.

"Can I get something for you drink?" She bit her lower lip and peered at him with a wary look in her eyes.

He'd screwed up things by holding her gaze too long. She couldn't suspect his motives or she'd be afraid of him. That would never work. He had to win her devotion.

"Coffee would be good, ma'am." He swallowed hard and summoned buried pain from the day he'd been forced to kill his wife to shut her up. He hadn't cried then, but he'd do it now if he must.

"I'm sorry if my staring makes you uncomfortable. It's just that you remind me so much of my baby sister. I really miss her." He brushed a fake tear from the corner of his eyes.

"Is okay." She touched his arm and smiled so sweetly he nearly groaned from the pleasure it brought him. Waiting for this woman was going to be a daunting task.

Closing his eyes a moment, he rested his hand on hers and added, "Bless you for your concern." Ugh. Now he sounded like a priest. What kind of crap just came out of his mouth?

Her eyes sparkled as she squeezed his hand. "You very welcome."

As she left to place his order, it struck him in the solar plexus. Religion... of course! That's how he'd get to her. He'd tap into memories of his dead wife's faith, painful as they were, and bring up everything about God that he could remember. Even the things that ultimately made him take her life. If religion would win this young woman over, then so be it. He could stomach it for a while if the end result would make her fully his.

Someone else delivered his breakfast. He gobbled it up without tasting it as he waited for her to come by and give him his check. He rubbed his hands on his jeans and smiled as she approached him.

"Pardon me, ma'am, but how do you pronounce your name?" He pointed at her nametag.

"Jovana. Jovana Trajkovski." She rang up the tab and returned with his change.

"What a beautiful name. I will pray for you. Would that be okay?" He slipped her a note with a five-dollar tip. Nothing threatening. Just enough encouragement to put her more at ease with him.

She blinked several times as if in shock. A smile slowly covered her face. "Yes. Is good."

He grinned in reply. Surely he would win this woman's heart. It was just a matter of time.

Chapter One

Jovana clocked out once the lunch crowd left. She smiled to herself and sighed. She'd just finished her first week on the job and already she'd met a man who was *simpatichen*, nice. He'd said something about his sister and missing her. She didn't understand the exact meaning of his words but knew the pain in his eyes meant that he was sad, so she responded with one of the phrases she knew well, "Is okay."

He must've understood her because he'd patted her hand and said, "Bless you." The kind look on his face told her this response was a compliment. She remembered years ago seeing a religious man on television say bless you as he touched the worshippers' heads. This man must be a religious man, too. But he was also very *mashko*, masculine, and he smelled so good -- like soap and spices -- that it made her pulse race when she stood near him. She closed her eyes for a moment and thought about what it would be like to kiss this man who didn't know her, yet treated her with such kindness.

As a new Christian she realized her budding faith hadn't erased her problems or her past, but getting to know a man with similar beliefs was something she yearned for. Something she wanted to believe in. His kindness and attitude told her that God was very important to him. She could tell from the look in his eyes that he was attracted to her. But other than handing a small note to her with her tip, he didn't make any moves on her, which she respected. A man who was able to control his urges was a man she wanted to know better. Plus, he didn't wear a wedding band, which meant he was available.

At first the man's friendliness made her a bit nervous, but then he'd mentioned prayer. Surely a man who had faith in God would be safe to get to know, right? At least he wasn't a gypsy, like her former boyfriend had been. Georg wanted nothing to do with God. He'd nearly killed her. At the time, Jovana didn't care about God either, so they were a good match until he started hurting her.

Her brother would not understand if he found out she'd met someone because of her past relationship with Georg. He would remember her past abuse and be afraid that she had met another man like him. As much as she hated to be deceptive because her brother had helped her so much, she would keep this one secret from him if she must. The incredible pull this man had on her was difficult to resist.

Now she needed to figure out who would read the note to her and not tell her brother. She carried a *rechnik* in her pocket to help her with words, but the Macedonian to English dictionary didn't help much when it came to translating sentences or concepts. It was better than nothing, so she would try it and see if the dictionary's translation would be useful.

She hid in the bathroom, and wrestled with translating the words on the paper until she grew so frustrated that tears filled her eyes. The handwritten words on the note he'd handed her were strung together with so many loops that it made the note indecipherable. Typed words were much easier to read that words written in cursive. She worried that she would never learn enough English to make friends or be understood by people other than her *bratko,* her brother.

A light tap on the door startled her. "You okay in there?"

"I am fine." This was another one of the few phrases she had perfected.

The faint sound of retreating footsteps told her the person had believed her and left. She splashed cool water on her face and looked in the mirror. While not as gaunt as she'd looked when she first lost her baby, she needed to gain more weight to look healthy. Pinching her cheeks to add some color, she exited the bathroom and grabbed her purse.

Her *shefe,* her boss, who happened to also be the restaurant manager, smiled and waved from across the room. Randy Strong was only a few years older than she was and so far he'd been very patient as she learned the many tasks required by her waitressing job. He also knew a little bit of Macedonian and Greek from working with her brother back when her brother had first moved to Arizona. But he was not skilled enough in either language for them to have a real conversation.

She would study English day and night if it would help her to communicate with the man who gave her the generous tip. The only reason she had a job in the first place was because her brother, Bojan, had recently purchased *The Diner* where she worked. Even though the United States economy slogged through a recession, he'd asked her to work for him because he could not find enough good help in their town.

Since she had wanted to leave Macedonia because of her painful past anyway, she was more than willing to come and help him get his new business established. In order for her to stay in the *Soedinetite Amerikanski* after Bojan's wedding, she needed to have a job and be able to support herself. Their arrangement had worked out perfectly... so far.

As she pulled on her jacket she couldn't help wondering... Were all Americans as friendly as the man she'd met that morning at breakfast? This was only her third week as a resident of Arizona. So far she enjoyed living in the high desert, but sometimes she missed her home country and her grandmother. Despite the painful sentiments she thanked God that she was able to stay with her brother's fiancée, Laney. She enjoyed helping the couple prepare for their long-awaited wedding.

Jovana offered her *shefe* a cursory wave. He gestured at her to come to him, so she did.

"Take this home with you." Randy offered a kind smile as he handed her a warm paper bag. The contents smelled heavenly, liked potatoes and salt. While he was not as attractive as the man she'd served that morning, he had a kind personality that she found hard to resist.

"*Eve ja dajende.*"

She giggled. He was trying so hard to speak her language correctly. She didn't have the heart to tell him when he used a wrong pronunciation or strung his words together incorrectly.

"*Blagodaram.* Thank you."

"*Molam.* You're welcome." He winked.

Peeking into the paper bag, she spied a Styrofoam container. She took a whiff and inhaled the scent of french fries. She glanced up and feigned a shocked expression. "You think I *slab*?"

Randy blinked. "No, I don't think you're a slob. Why would giving you fries make you a slob?"

She winked at him and used a pet phrase he'd taught her. "Gotcha, Man. Slab mean thin, or weak. Is funny, yes?"

He laughed and said, "Yep, you got me." He eyed her from head to foot and added with a smile, "You're not too thin by American standards. I think you're just right."

She felt her cheeks warm at the compliment. "Is American womens looking like chicken legs and bony ribs?"

Randy chuckled louder. "I have no idea what you are saying."

"American womens is thin, yes, like how you say... skeleton?"

"Some. But nowadays most American women are a bit overweight."

She teased him by frowning and glancing at him from the corner of her eye. "You say I am fat? Is this true, Ron-dee?"

That statement couldn't be true because she didn't have an extra pound on her, though she wanted to remedy that. The fries would certainly help.

His puzzled expression made her grin. She pressed her fingertips against her lips.

"No. Not at all." He flashed a contrite smile that revealed perfect white teeth.

The tiny flutter in her stomach made her pause. She enjoyed playing the word games with Randy, but she could never date her boss. He'd told her he wanted to learn her language better so she teased him about it every chance she got. Sometimes she would say something funny just to see if he knew the meaning of her words. Most of the time he didn't get her jokes, but he was learning.

"Thank you, again, boss man." She winked at him to let him know she wasn't offended.

"See you tomorrow. Enjoy the fries."

Jovana popped a few in her mouth and chewed. Delicious. "How much must I pay?"

"Nothing. It was a botched order. I would have had to throw them out anyway."

She had no clue what he meant by botched, but she did understand that nothing meant she didn't have to pay and that throw away meant he would have put them in the trash. Americans wasted so much food. When she thought about how she'd nearly starved to death when Georg had abandoned her in Macedonia, it made the fries taste even more delicious. She opened the front door and waved over her shoulder. "*Chao.* Bye-bye."

Glancing around the parking lot for her ride, Jovana smiled when she saw Laney's SUV parked off to the side. While Laney waited she chatted on her cell phone, most likely with Bojan. The moment she saw Jovana she honked the *kola's* horn and waved.

Americans had such nice cars. She wished she could afford one of her own. Even an old one would suit her fine. Her *bratko* had offered to buy her a car, but she wanted to earn her keep. Besides, she wasn't ready yet to take the driver's test. She didn't read English and she doubted they'd have a Macedonian version of the test. Better to accept rides for now and be grateful she didn't have to walk.

Once Laney and Bojan were married and her brother moved into Laney's house, Jovana planned to rent his fifth wheel from him and then she could walk to work. He'd told her that the rent for the space was only two hundred American dollars per month. Since he owned the fifth wheel he refused to let her pay for anything else. By the end of her first week of work she'd earned almost that much in tips, so paying her bills shouldn't be a problem.

Jovana stepped over to the passenger door of Laney's car and climbed inside. She couldn't contain her smile as she thought about the many ways God had blessed her since she'd arrived in the United States. And today had been an amazing Friday morning. She'd tricked her boss again and she'd captured a handsome admirer's attention all in the same day.

Laney tapped on the face of her cell phone and turned it off, then returned her phone to the front pocket of her purse.

Laney glanced at her and smiled wide. "You look tickled pink. Did you have a good day?"

"Tickled pink?" Jovana felt her cheeks to see if they were hot. "This means emotion? I mix up sayings."

"Yes, it means happy." Laney laughed. "I can't believe how much you've learned in just a few weeks."

"Is very good, yes?" She reached into her pocket and fingered the note. Maybe Laney would help her translate the message.

"That's excellent. Your *bratko* was a slow learner." Laney chuckled. "Then again, he might have been faking it just to spend more time with me."

Jovana loved how Laney spoke slowly and enunciated every word to give her time to translate the words in her head. While she studied the language every night before bed, she had a ways to go before she'd become fluent enough to be functional. "You say my *bratko* do something faking to be with you? What this means?"

"Faking it means that he played dumb with me. You know, like acting stupid?"

She couldn't help smirking. "How you know he fake stupid?"

"Ooh, I'm not telling Boki what you just said." Laney snickered as she pulled out of the parking lot.

"Is good you not tell my brother." Jovana touched Laney's arm. "You help something, please?"

"Sure. What do you need?"

Jovana waited until Laney pulled onto the dirt road leading up the mountain to her house and handed Laney the paper. She prayed that it was a good message. "I cannot read note."

Laney checked the rearview mirror and pulled off to the side. Opening the piece of paper, Laney smiled and read the words out loud. "Keep up the good work. See you next week."

"That is all?"

Laney nodded and her brows lifted in question. "What did you hope it would say?"

"Nothing. Note comes with tip. I could not read words with this writing."

"Sounds like the person appreciated your service. That's a good thing."

Laney glanced over her shoulder, then drove slowly to avoid potholes, something they had an abundance of in the town where Jovana's parents lived outside of Skopje.

Jovana did her best to hide her disappointment. She had hoped the note would contain something a bit more romantic. She supposed she should be grateful that it didn't say anything personal that Laney might tell her brother. "Yes. Is very good."

*****

Randy resisted the urge to hit his head on the counter and punish himself for acting so stupid. He'd promised himself he would not hit on the boss's sister and here he was winking at her and teasing her like a love sick kid from junior high. Could his attraction to her be any more obvious? His boss would kill him if he tried to date her, especially after he'd promised Bojan he would look out for his sister and make sure that no strange men put the moves on her. So here he was doing the very thing he was supposed to help her avoid.

But try as he might, he couldn't seem to stop flirting with her. When she wasn't at work he couldn't get her out of his mind. Those lips of hers reminded him of Angelina Jolie's and that accent that clung to every word she spoke gave him the most delightful shivers. She was so feminine and modest, very unlike most of the young women he'd met over the years. A few of those women had tried to get him into bed, but they weren't successful. So far he'd managed to keep himself pure by avoiding pushy women. Plus, he refused to date and fall in love with a woman who didn't go to church.

No doubt being raised in another country had influenced Jovana in a positive way. Bojan had told him once that he had been raised in the Orthodox tradition. He also mentioned in passing that Jovana had put her faith in Christ last year. That encouraged him, though they had yet to discuss matters of faith. So far she had not brought it up, and the timing never seemed right for him to ask her about her beliefs. One day soon they would address this. For now he just wanted to observe her.

He just couldn't imagine Jovana pushing herself on a man. She acted too shy and polite to be aggressive. And that sexy accent of hers was enough to make him drool. Sometimes he would ask her something just to hear her say his name. She always pronounced it wrong, but it sounded so cute when she said Ron-dee that he would never correct her.

There was also something vulnerable about her that made her all the more attractive to him. Like he would with a child, he longed to protect her from the ugly things in life. It really bugged him that a middle-aged guy watched her work that morning long after he'd finished his breakfast. Sure, she was pretty, but normally that didn't make a customer sit and sip coffee for a full thirty minutes after finishing their meal just to watch their waitress serve other customers.

She'd obviously enjoyed the attention because each time the man spoke to her she flushed bright red. Plus, he noticed her peeking at the man from the corner of her eye when she was in the dining area. A sensation -- like hot metal searing his chest -- burned through him when he thought of anyone else wanting her and possibly taking advantage of her innocence.

He tried to brush the disturbing thought from his mind. No doubt the man acted that way with a lot of women. From the way he watched her, he seemed like a real playboy. Unfortunately, someone as sweet and innocent as Jovana would undoubtedly get pulled in by his charm.

Something in his gut told him the man was bad news, but he didn't want to overreact and say anything to her or to her brother just yet. He'd keep an eye on the guy just in case... but figured the man was passing through town. He didn't recognize him from the surrounding community, so he saw no sense in getting Bojan riled up over the situation.

How he wished Jovana would look at him the way she'd gazed at the stranger that morning. His stomach burned with jealousy when he thought about how she responded to that playboy. Should he say something to warn her? Part of him really wanted to, but the more reasonable part decided to let things blow over. That way he wouldn't risk upsetting her over what was probably nothing.

One thing he knew for sure about Jovana was that she did *not* want Bojan protecting her. She made it clear during one of her recent arguments with her brother. Randy couldn't help overhearing them even though they yelled at each other in Macedonian.

The phone rang back in the kitchen. Randy went to answer it knowing in advance it had to be Bojan. No one else had the new number and it wasn't in the phone book yet. "What's up, Boss?"

"Is Jovanichka at work?"

"No, I let her go home early. Things slowed down so she asked Laney to come pick her up a half an hour before her shift ended. Why? Did you need her for something?"

"I must talk to her about family stuffs. I will try house. *Fala.*"

Uh-oh. Not family issues again.

He prayed Bojan's grandmother hadn't passed away this time. When she'd gotten sick a few months ago they all thought for sure she wasn't going to make it, but Bojan had said his grandmother was tough. He hoped things were okay with her because if she were sick, that would take him out of town right before their wedding. In just a few weeks his boss planned to take his new bride on their honeymoon to Paris, the most romantic place on earth.

Randy sighed. He had saved up money for the past three years so he could buy a house and spoil his future bride. So far he hadn't met the right woman. *Not unless Jovana was the one.*

As much as he wanted Jovana to be attracted to him, it looked like God would have to do a miraculous change in her heart for that to happen. From what he could tell she didn't see him as anything more than an older brother. She'd pretty much said that the one time he dared to hint that he might like her the way a man likes a woman. She'd even referred to him as her *bratko* in Christ. And while he knew that all Christians were brothers and sisters in Christ, he couldn't help suspecting that there was a hidden meaning in her words. Otherwise she wouldn't have looked him straight in the eyes when she'd made her declaration the other day.

Randy shuddered, jarring him from his musing. A shiver pebbled his skin and the hair rose on his arms. The sense that something evil lurked nearby made him rub them several times, and a strong desire to pray grabbed hold of him. Without knowing the exact reason, he uttered a prayer for Bojan, his family, and especially his little sister, Jovana. If any of them needed protection, they'd get it from the heavenly hosts if he had anything to say about it.

He waited until the frightening sensation passed. As he grabbed the garbage bag and tied the sack, he finished up his prayer for peace. With a grunt, he lifted the heavy load and hauled it over to the Dumpster in the alley. From the corner of his eye he saw something slip around the corner of the restaurant. Whether it was an animal or a person was hard to tell from his peripheral vision because it moved so fast. After tossing the bag, he walked over to the side of building, but he didn't find anything obviously out of place or anyone hanging around in the alley.

He shuddered and told himself to stop being so paranoid. But just in case, he touched his S&W 9MM to make sure it was still secured at his waist. Every morning he got up and right after he dressed for the day he added the gun and slipped it inside the holster. He concealed it under a vest so no one could rob him and get away with it this time. His concealed weapons permit allowed him to carry the needed protection. He thanked God regularly for the Constitution and his right to bear arms.

The back door banged as it slammed shut behind him.

Without thinking, Randy grabbed his 9MM and spun on his heels. Clutching his weapon with both hands, he crouched, ready to shoot. His heart hammered so hard it hurt like he was having an actual heart attack.

Shep jumped back, his arms raised in surrender. Relief washed over him like a gust of cool wind and he lowered his gun. "Don't freaking scare me like that! I could've shot you."

Shep squinted and fisted his hands on his hips. "Scare you? What the heck are you doing out here with a gun?"

"Just taking out the trash like you're supposed to do. It was overflowing onto the cement floor in the kitchen. So where were you?"

"In the bathroom. I am allowed to use it, right boss?"

He grunted his agreement. "So what are you doing scaring the flipping stuffing out of me?"

"No need to get jumpy. I just wondered where the schedule was posted. I can't find it and I need to ask you for a day off next week."

"You can't find it because I haven't posted it yet. Just fill out your request and put it in the box like everyone else." Randy forced himself to take a deep breath and relax. Shep wasn't the enemy. He was asking a simple question, which required a simple answer.

"So why do you carry a gun? Because of what happened in Tucson?"

"Maybe." He sighed and squeezed the back of his neck, which now ached. "Probably."

"Was it bad?" Shep squinted at him like he wanted to know more, but didn't dare ask.

"The worst." He rubbed his forehead, not sure he wanted to share much with this man he hardly knew, but thinking it might benefit him to talk about it at the same time.

"I'll bet. For you to pull a gun on me--"

"Sorry about my reaction, but I get jumpy when I'm alone."

After being robbed and left for dead, he swore to himself that he'd never be vulnerable again. If he'd been armed he would've been able to defend himself during the robbery and protect his female employee. Then one of those robbers wouldn't have been able to sneak in the back door and nail him in the skull with a tire iron while the other guy raped the waitress who had stayed late that night to help him close the restaurant. He could have protected her and chased them off. *If* he'd had a gun...

"The boss had said something about an armed robbery up in Tucson that happened before he hired you to run *The Diner*." Shep pulled out a cigarette and a lighter and lit up. He took a long drag, and slowly exhaled. "He said you were a good manager but nearly got killed at that Greek place he used to own."

"What else did he tell you?"

"Not much. Just that after the robbery you quit for a while and then he sold the place."

"I couldn't stomach working there after what happened to Melody. She didn't deserve that." His voice cracked. He suppressed the ache welling up before it spilled over and he embarrassed himself.

Shep blew several smoke circles and looked at him from the corner of his eye. "You didn't deserve to get your head cracked open either."

Randy clenched his fists as the acrid smoke irritated his nostrils. "But she got it worse. I could hear those dogs raping her and I couldn't move or do a thing about it. I couldn't even open my eyes."

His employee watched him, silent as he took another drag. This time Shep was careful to blow the smoke away from him when he exhaled.

Randy swallowed his tears. When he thought about her cries for help he got choked up all over again from the guilt. Would the pain from that night ever lessen?

His employee pulled another drag from his cigarette and released it through his nostrils in little puffs. The guy reminded him of Puff the Magic Dragon. "You ever miss Tucson?"

He rubbed the back of his skull. At least once a month he got a wicked headache in the same spot where the tire iron had knocked him out. "Nah. I like Sierra Vista better. It's smaller and there isn't that much crime. Not that I know of anyway."

Shep stared at him for a moment then glanced away. He finished his cigarette and ground the butt under his heel. Without saying a word, he walked toward the back door and stepped inside.

Randy's skull throbbed again. He winced as he watched Shep close the door. The enemy of his soul seemed to enjoy torturing him with memories that most of the time he successfully blocked out. What he thought he'd seen in the alley was probably nothing.

Just his imagination running amok again.

His former pastor would call his overreaction a symptom of Post Traumatic Stress Disorder. He didn't know what he suffered from, but he hated feeling on edge from every little noise. His symptoms were the worst late at night. Probably because that was the time of day the robbery had occurred. Things were always safer in broad daylight. That was the reason he'd taken on this new job. *The Diner* was never open at night. So far there had been no daytime crimes reported in Sierra Vista other than the shooting he'd read about that happened at the park in the middle of the afternoon last week.

He hoped the shooting was a freak situation, because even though he had a gun and wore it everywhere he went, he still prayed he'd never have to use it. Closing his eyes, he asked God to keep him from ever having to kill anyone. But, Heaven forbid, if he did have to use his gun to protect a young woman like Jovana, he wouldn't hold anything back.

He'd make that person regret ever being born.

Chapter Two

Jovana stared out the window at the foothills as they slowly approached Laney's house. The size of the structure made her parents' grand home in Macedonia look like a shack. She marveled at the wealth all around her and wondered if she would ever fit in. She loved America so far, but the culture was difficult to understand. The people had so many sayings that made no sense. Her *bratko* called them idioms. He even showed her a booklet he was given called *Idioms for Idiots*. Her brother was anything but an idiot, but the title still intrigued her because she didn't see why anyone would want to buy a book that suggested the reader had to be an idiot to read it.

"Look, Boki's following us." Laney grinned and directed Jovana to look in the rearview mirror. "Is he the typical overprotective older brother, or what?"

Sure enough, her brother's yellow Hummer H2 crept up the dirt road behind them, kicking up a swirl of dust as it approached at a brisk pace. Apparently the potholes didn't bother him much. It annoyed her that he had followed them home again after promising to not hover. Hopefully he hadn't heard about the man who gave her the tip.

She tried to change the subject and asked, "You have date tonight?"

Laney smiled. "I can't believe how fast you are learning English. No, we don't have a date. I'm not sure why he's stopping by. Normally he calls me first."

Jovana watched as Laney alternated between driving up the road and checking her cell phone for messages. Thankfully she only drove about 10 kilometers per hour.

"No flashing light indicating I missed any calls." She tapped a button with her nail and her phone lit up. "Ah, that's because he texted me. Can you tell me what it says?"

Jovana caught the phone that Laney gently tossed at her. "I try."

She peered at the message and tried to decipher it, which wasn't too difficult as her brother used a few Macedonian words in his message, plus it was typed and not handwritten like the note. "He says he must talk to me about family stuffs."

"Do you have any idea what he is talking about?"

Jovana couldn't help smiling at the expression on Laney's face. "No."

"Hmmm..."

Laney's wrinkled forehead looked so cute. She could see why Bojan had fallen for the young woman. Ironically, they looked alike but Laney was taller than her, though not as tall as her brother. They appeared similar enough to be related except that Jovana's build was almost tiny in comparison. And Laney had blue eyes, not brown like her own.

Except for the blue eyes the color of *borovinkas*, blueberries, Laney looked like she could be from Macedonia. Bojan had mentioned their similarities had drawn him to Laney when he first saw her. He'd also been drawn to the sad expression in Laney's eyes.

No doubt that sadness reminded him of those difficult times they shared when they were young. Jovana had many bad experiences with boys even before she met Georg and ran away from her family. Her brother had taken it personally when she went missing the last time, but had since forgiven her.

The phone vibrated in her hand, startling her. She almost dropped it on the floor. She checked and saw Bojan's picture appear on the screen so she pushed the green button.

"*Alo*?" She decided to speak to him in their native tongue so Laney wouldn't understand her if she started correcting him for what he was doing. She would keep her voice calm, but her meaning would be clear. Boki was starting to get on her nerves. He was smothering her.

"Hello, my dear *sestra*. How are you?"

"I am good, my overprotective *bratko*. I told you before to stop pestering me. You do not need to follow us home. You said you would not do that to me anymore."

"I was not following for that reason. It is important that I speak with you in person."

"Okay, I will speak to you, but we will talk in private in case I get angry with you."

"You won't. I am only offering to do what is best. You know I worry about you."

Jovana rolled her eyes as Laney pulled into the garage and turned off the engine. Good thing her *bratko* couldn't see her gesture or he might be offended.

Laney touched Jovana's arm and whispered, "Is he giving you a hard time again?"

Jovana did not understand how time could be hard so she shrugged. So many sayings made no sense. It would take her forever to understand so many things.

"*Chao*." She pushed the button and ended their conversation. Handing Laney the cell phone, she said, "*Fala*, thank you."

"Is no problem." Laney imitated Boki's favorite saying and did such a great imitation that Jovana felt a giggle tickling her throat.

She pressed her fingers to her lips and tried to contain her mirth, but failed.

Boki pulled up next to them in the garage and killed the engine. Always the gentleman, he opened Laney's door first. She watched her brother cradle Laney's face and lower his mouth to hers. Her face heated at the sight of their tender kissing. Would a man ever love her like that?

How she missed the warm, tingling sensations from a man's touch. But despite her occasional loneliness, she knew she was better off single than with a man who would abuse her as savagely as Georg had done. The sad thing was she had been so sure that Georg cared about her. And he'd been an amazing lover despite the fact that he'd rarely kissed her. Not that she should be resurrecting those memories right now. They only made the pain more intense because the truth was he'd turned on her after telling her that he'd loved her like nobody else ever would.

At first he seemed to fulfill that promise. Then something changed between them. She suspected it was her first unplanned pregnancy that resulted in a miscarriage. A year later after beating her severely, he'd gotten her pregnant again and in his anger left her on the streets to starve when she was with child. She had been about seven months pregnant. If he had truly loved her like he swore he did then he would never have beaten her and treated her so poorly that she ultimately lost their child. Some days the pain was so intense from the loss that she wished Georg dead. She hated to admit that to herself, because it wasn't very Christian, but it was the truth.

Laney giggled and finally broke free from Bojan's kisses. They touched foreheads for a moment and stared into each other's eyes. Jovana resisted the urge to release an obnoxious sigh. Whenever her brother and Laney got together it was as if no one else existed.

He shut the door on the driver's side and walked Laney to the back door inside the open garage. He then rounded the car to open Jovana's door and offered his hand to assist her like she was royalty. It had been almost nine months since her baby died and still her *bratko* treated her like she would break.

Rather than being crabby with him as he no doubt expected, she smiled and received his hand, which elicited a double eyebrow lift from him. "Are you feeling okay?" he asked in Macedonian.

"I am well, but would be better if you did not hover so much," she replied in her native tongue.

Laney opened the back door and slipped inside her house as the electric garage door slowly slid shut and enveloped them in darkness. Jovana couldn't restrain the shiver that zinged up her spine.

Bojan had his hand on her arm, so he felt her quiver. "I am concerned for you, Jovanichka. I am worried you will be afraid if you are left alone when we leave for our honeymoon in a few weeks."

"I'll be fine." She rubbed her arms and did not look at him as her eyes adjusted.

"You are a terrible liar." He touched her chin and tipped her head up so she had to look at him.

She avoided his gaze. "You are too protective. It is not helping my confidence."

"Our mother and father asked me to watch over you. After thinking you were kidnapped and dead for over five years, how could you expect any less?"

"But I am a grown woman, my *bratko*."

"Yes, you are, and a very attractive woman at that. From what I hear, several of your customers have already taken notice."

She squinted at him. "Did Ron-dee tell you this?"

Bojan laughed. "No. But Shep said that you are improving business so much that the number of daily customers has doubled since you starting working there."

"It is not because of me, I assure you." Jovana suppressed a smile when she thought of the man who had given her a five-dollar tip for an inexpensive breakfast and a cup of coffee.

He chucked her chin. "Don't be so sure. You are a beautiful lady."

Her cheeks heated. Now she could see his face, and her eyes were adjusting to the darkness. "*Blagodaram*. Thank you."

Laney flicked the garage light on and the sudden change made them both wince. Bojan rubbed his eyes. "Because you are so beautiful I want to make sure you are safe when Laney and I are in Paris."

"I thought I was going to stay in your fifth wheel."

"I have decided to lend it to a friend for the two weeks we are in Europe. He is going camping up in Mesa for the same two weeks we are gone and he needed a camper. I told him he could take it as long as he brings it back the day before we return. You can move into my fifth wheel after we get back. We want you to take care of the dogs and house plants while we are gone. Are you willing to do this?"

"Of course. But how will I get to work?"

"That's the thing I need to talk to you about. I am going to ask Randy to stay here with you and make sure you are safe. He will drive you to work and bring you home every day."

"Randy? You mean my boss? He would stay here with me during the night?"

"Yes, then you won't be left alone. He'll stay in a different room, of course, so you'll have privacy. Laney and I don't want to worry about your safety while we are on our honeymoon."

"You don't need to have someone babysit me."

"It will not be babysitting. It is for companionship as well as protection."

"I don't understand why you want to do this. Of all the people to ask to stay here with me, why my boss? That's just wrong, Boki."

"Maybe it seems wrong, but he is one of the few people I trust. Plus, this is a huge house and I am sure he is not going to harm you here or anywhere else for that matter."

"He is nice and he treats me with respect, but I would feel strange with someone in the house other than Laney. Especially someone I work with who is also a man. How well do you know Randy?"

"I know him well enough to know he will keep you safe and watch out for you. Better to feel strange than get hurt when you are left alone. Did I ever tell you what happened to Laney here when we were dating? She was attacked in her own home."

"Yes. She told me the story, but she said the man knew her. He was not some random man off the street." She rested her fists on her hips. Sometimes her brother could be too paranoid.

"There are illegals frequently crossing over this mountain. Sometimes they knock on the windows and ask for water. Some people have been robbed."

"I will call the police if that happens." She crossed her arms. She wasn't the idiot he seemed to think she was. She knew enough about American customs to know that dialing 9-1-1 would bring the police to her rescue in minutes.

"But, Jovana, you know when you get nervous you don't speak very well. How will you talk to the police if you are frightened?" The sincerity in his voice made her pause.

She'd forgotten about that. And her Spanish was worse than her English. "Of course, you are right. I did not think of my limitations."

"Good. I knew talking to you in person would help you understand."

She had to remember he was just trying to provide support for her in his absence. He knew she couldn't exactly call him on his cell phone in Paris. And she would not want to interrupt their marital bliss unless it was an emergency. Her parents had returned to Macedonia to be with their *baba* because of her recent illness, so she couldn't call them. At least Randy knew some of her language.

"I do understand, my dear *bratko*. Thank you for thinking of my well being. The Lord has given you wisdom to help me when I am too bull-headed to see that I need it."

"You are not bull-headed, though I saw horns a few minutes ago when you were upset with me."

She swatted his arm, but not hard. "I do not have horns."

He laughed and opened the door to let them into Laney's house. Before she stepped inside, she gasped. "What if Randy does not agree to your request? Will you still go to Paris?"

Bojan winked. "Do not concern yourself with such trivial matters. Your big brother will take care of you. Your boss will not mind helping me, of this I am certain."

Something about her brother's smile made her stomach twist. He could be so aggravating. "But you said you have not asked him yet. What if he says no?"

"If he refuses I will offer to pay him enough to make him reconsider. I am his boss."

"You would not do that!"

"You worry too much." Bojan smiled and called to Laney in the other room in English, "Honey, you think Randy refuse for to stay with Jovanichka in house when we go to Paris?"

Laney laughed. "No. Definitely not."

She nibbled on her lip and stared at her brother's amused expression. Something weird was going on that she didn't know about, and it involved her boss. But what could it be?

They better not try to set her up with him. It would be sinful if she and her boss got into a compromising position, but she highly doubted that would happen. She didn't like him in a romantic sense. He was too nice. Plus, he was a good Christian and a rather intimidating one at that.

She hadn't known the Lord very long but she knew that her boss was a good man who worshipped Jesus. Even though she knew God had forgiven her past sins, she also knew her boss was too good for her. He would never be interested in a woman with her shameful past. She didn't know what to do with a man of faith who was respectful and sincere. A man who lived what he believed.

But a man with a charming smile like the one who'd given her the five-dollar tip? A man like him, she could handle. Her body tingled when she thought about seeing him again.

*****

Randy had just kicked off his shoes and plopped on the couch when his phone rang. "Hello?"

"Randy, this is Bojan. May I speak in person for you tonight?"

He rubbed his eyes and yawned. "I'm kinda tired."

"This will not take much time." Bojan's words sounded clipped.

"Okay. When can you get here?"

"Five minutes. Is very important for me to speak tonight."

"All right. I'll be here. You remember how to get to my place?"

"Yes, I am right down street. *Chao.*"

A surge of adrenaline shot through him and suddenly Randy felt wide awake. His boss was coming over about an important matter. A lump of guilt filled his throat. Had his boss caught him looking at Jovana? Was he coming over to correct him for being too friendly with her?

His heart pumped hard as he zipped through his small apartment and straightened things up. Sweat trickled down his forehead and rolled into his eyes as he scrubbed the sink and counter top until it sparkled. He wiped his face with a paper towel and dropped the damp cloth in the kitchen trash.

Someone knocked on his apartment door. As he went to answer it he prayed for calmness to come over him so he would not get defensive if he disagreed with his boss. He had no idea why Bojan wanted to see him. The fact that his boss came over at night and insisted on talking in person made Randy's hands tremble even though he hadn't done anything wrong.

"Hi. Come on in." Randy moved out of the way and shut the door the moment Bojan stepped inside. His boss didn't seem angry at all. In fact, he looked pretty happy. So why did he insist on coming over?

"Many thanks for have me over last minute."

"No problem. Would you like some coffee?"

"Is too late for coffee. Plus stuff you make put hairs on chest." Bojan laughed. He slapped Randy on the back and directed him toward the couch.

Randy sat next to his boss and rested his palms on his knees. He had no reason to be nervous, but that didn't stop him from trembling. "Okay, boss, I'm all ears."

Bojan laughed. "Americans have strange... how you say... expressions? I know this does not mean you have many ears. Does saying all ears mean you listen?"

"Yes, it does. Very good." Randy popped his knuckles as he waited.

His boss shuddered. "That sound is *prechi komu* for me."

"Pretchy, huh?" That was the first time he'd heard that saying.

"Mean the sound you make bother me, or as American slang say, the sound bugs me. This makes no sense that Americans say bugs is word for bother."

"I think it does." Randy chuckled. "Have you ever had a fly buzzing around your head?"

Bojan nodded.

"Picture this. A fly is a bug, right? So the annoying things it does like landing on you and pestering you is where the word bugging comes from."

"How you know this?" Bojan's brow wrinkled.

"I don't know for sure. I just figured out the meaning while we were talking. I could be wrong, though. Won't be the first time."

Bojan tilted his head. "We must talk slangs later. I want for learn to speak slang phrases good."

"Sure. Just make sure I'm home first so you don't waste your time stopping by."

His boss nodded and his expression grew serious. "Now we must talk about reason for visit. Is this okay for you?"

Randy swallowed the peach-pit sized lump in his throat. "Sure."

"Is very good. We must speak of Jovanichka."

His heart pounding, Randy wondered if his boss had suspected his growing feelings for her. He answered slowly, "What about her?"

19

"You face is much red. Why is her name make for you blush?"

"Um... I..."

"Is Laney correct? You like my *sestra*?"

"Ah..."

Bojan pinned him with his gaze. "Is okay for this if respect for Jovana is true."

Randy swiped the sweat beading on his forehead before it rolled into his eyes. "I do respect her."

"Is very good. Now I say why I must speak tonight."

He nodded at his boss and relief washed over him like a cooling mist. Bojan wasn't upset about him liking Jovana. But why not? That unanswered question made his muscles knot up again.

"We travel to Paris after wedding and my *sestra* stay in home but is my problem for Jovanichka being alone in *kukja*."

Huh? "Are you saying that you don't want Jovana home alone while you are out of town?

"Yes. We ask for you help. Can you do this?"

"Do what?" Randy wiped his sweaty palms on his jeans.

"Stay in house for Jovanichka is not alone."

"I'm confused about your meaning. If you want me to stay in Laney's house while you are gone, where will Jovana stay?"

"Same house."

His heart pitter pattered at the idea of being in the same home with Jovana for two entire weeks. "I don't think I can do that, boss. I'm sorry, but Christians are supposed to avoid the appearance of evil. You know that."

"Is not true evil. Is... how you say... necessary evil. My *sestra* is safe for you in home. Is no problem for you stay same place. If people ask, you say I pay you for protect *sestra*. Like... hmm... how you say... like bodyguard?"

"You want me to be her bodyguard? Is she royalty or something?"

Bojan's eyes turned to slits as he laughed. "No, but is good for you respect like she is princess."

"So why does she need watching?" He didn't think he could handle being so close to her for that amount of time. He already had dreams about kissing her lips and holding her close. What would he do about those fantasies if she actually liked him back? So far she hadn't given him any indication she'd felt that way about him. Maybe he worried for nothing.

"You know story of attack?"

"The one that happened to Laney while I still lived in Tucson?"

"Yes. Man attack Laney in home. Is not safe for woman in big house alone. Is one reason for having Jovanichka move to Arizona. This and for her bridesmaid duty in wedding."

"It is pretty isolated on the foothills. The neighbors' homes aren't close enough for anyone to hear you scream if you're in trouble."

"Yes, is very true." Bojan touched his arm. "Please do this."

His body tensed when he thought about spending so much time alone with Jovana. Even her name was sexy enough to elicit a response from him whenever he heard it. He knew his boss's plan was a bad idea given his extreme attraction to her. Plus, she was a new Christian and she seemed pretty vulnerable, so she might not understand his reasoning if he kept a firm distance for both of their sakes.

"How does Jovana feel about this?"

"At first she worry, but now is no problem."

"What did she worry about?" Did she feel attracted to him, too?

"She worry for man stay in house and how looks for people who know Christ to see man in home and she is not married. I tell her no reason for worry about this. I tell her you are good man and would not do things for to make her worry."

"Of course she would be safe with me." He'd kissed several women, but had done nothing more than that even though some women had tried to persuade him to loosen up. Of course, he'd thought about doing more. He'd be a liar if he tried to pretend he'd never thought about having sex.

"I see how you look for my sister with kind eyes. You have feelings for Jovanichka that is more than for friends, yes?"

He swallowed hard. How much should he admit? "I do care for her as more than a... friend."

"Is good. Laney think you good match for Jovana. But Jovana is not ready for boyfriend. She have bad experience in Macedonia with man and needs for to heal from scars."

"I wouldn't try anything. You can trust me there." But what if she tried something with him?

"That is true. I ask God for wisdom and He says to me for ask you for help."

"He did?" *God, what did you do that for?*

"Yes." Bojan rubbed his forehead. "Is hard for believe God tells me you?"

"Yes, um, no, um... I don't know. I guess so."

"Is reason for me worry?" Bojan's piercing gaze made him nervous.

He closed his eyes so Bojan couldn't see the doubt he felt reflected in his expression. "No."

Lord, help him. If he did this for his boss then he would need added strength to resist temptation. While she might not be interested in him now, that could change if they spent enough time in the same home. He knew that all too well from his youth.

His older sister had a friend who would spend the night just about every weekend. As they grew older he found himself in several

21

uncomfortable situations when she was in their house that changed the way he thought about her. Once the door hadn't closed all the way and he'd seen Jennifer's friend, Liz, half undressed. Thankfully she hadn't seen him, but seeing her braless for just a few seconds still burned an image in his mind that he fought for years after that. Not to mention the intense crush he had developed on her -- or actually, her body -- as a result. She never reciprocated his feelings, of course, probably due to his younger age.

What would he do if Jovana pranced around the house half-dressed?

Bojan tapped his arm. "Why you not answer question?"

"What question?"

"I ask for you drive for work and bring *sestra* to diner. Can you do this?"

"Of course."

"Is very good." Bojan stood. "I tell Jovanichka you do this. *Blagodaram.*"

"*Molam.*"

After Bojan left, Randy closed his eyes and took a deep, shaky breath. God knew his weakness for this woman. His desire for her that defied explanation. He had never felt this way before about any woman. It was almost unhealthy how much he thought about Jovana and how he wanted to be with her all the time. Was this some sort of warped test he was being given to see if he would do the right thing by her? So far he hadn't had sex, but if there was one woman in this world who could make him forget his convictions, it would be Jovana.

Those pretty doe eyes of hers always drew him in when she spoke and the way she looked into his eyes made him breathless. And her sexy accent made him shiver with delight from just hearing her speak. He sometimes found it difficult to think when he was around her. Here he was, twenty-six years old, and she made him feel like he was back at the junior high summer camp the year he got saved. He'd fallen in love with one of the camp counselors and with Jesus all in the same week.

Jovana had told him when she started working at *The Diner* that she'd just turned twenty-three in September, but she didn't look a day over nineteen or twenty. Except for her eyes. Every once in awhile they looked tired and... sad, like she'd been through a lot. Maybe he'd ask her about that sometime so he could pray for her. He longed to know her heart.

His flesh warred with his spirit the more he thought about being alone in the same house with her and living like they were a married couple for two weeks. Being in different rooms would do little good at helping him to not think about her being so close by while he slept... if he slept.

Someday he hoped to show her that he cared for her as more than a friend. Then he'd see how she felt about a possible relationship with him. But until Bojan and Laney returned, he would have to keep a healthy distance. Then when he moved back to his apartment he might risk asking her on a date if he thought there was a chance she'd say yes.

However, the more he thought about the complications that could result from him dating an employee, the more he decided to avoid it. Her brother had sponsored her so that she could stay in the United States on her visa. She couldn't get a job anywhere else because of her limited proficiency in English. And with decent paying jobs being scarce these days, he couldn't exactly afford to just up and quit his job either. Plus, he felt a sense of obligation to his boss. He didn't want to work anywhere else.

This arrangement Bojan had made for him would be hard, but he'd find a way to manage.

He had no choice.

Chapter Three

Several days had passed before she saw the man again who had given her the generous tip, the one she had felt so drawn to for no particular reason. This morning he sat at the same table and watched her as she served her customers.

While the attention felt a bit unnerving, she savored it at the same time. Being abused for so many years by Georg and living in darkness had really damaged her inner strength. Knowing that a man found her attractive enough to sit and watch her for hours gave her a sense of power that she didn't know she possessed. It soothed her in a profound way.

Turning in his direction, she captured his attention and smiled. "More coffee?"

"Sure, honey." He caressed her with his gaze as she leaned close and poured him a refill.

"Much coffee is not good for you heart." She tapped her chest with her free hand. "Make this pound hard and hands shake."

He reached for her hand and held it. "You're trembling. Do I make your heart pound?"

"No." A nervous giggle escaped from her lips. She gently extracted her hand from his.

"Well, being near you makes my heart pound. The effect of coffee is nothing compared to how you make me feel, honey." He smiled and held her gaze.

She found herself gazing back at him and her heart fluttered. He was definitely interested in her. If there had been any doubt in her mind before, it no longer existed. "Thank you, sir."

"Please, call me Kurt." He peered at her as he sipped coffee from his cup. He obviously waited for her response.

"Okay, Kurt. Thank you."

"I love how my name sounds when you say it. What language do you speak? Other than English, I mean." His gaze drifted to her lips several times as he waited for her answer.

"Macedonian. I speak Greek also." Her neck heated as she imagined kissing him. She hadn't been tempted in a long time, so why did this stranger appeal to her so much? She shouldn't be attracted to a man she didn't know just because he had an amazing smile and paid attention to her.

He slipped her a ten-dollar bill as he stood. "Thanks for making my morning sweeter, honey. I promise I will stop by again. Miss me until I return." He winked and grabbed his jacket.

She watched him walk out, speechless. Did all American men show their interest so plainly? She didn't see him flirting with any of the other waitresses at the diner. He only acted that way with her. And ironically, she sensed that she *would* miss the guy. He was such a mystery. Or at least she'd miss the attention he gave her. The thought was unsettling. At first, Georg had given her a lot of attention, too. Then his attention morphed until it bordered on possessiveness.

Glancing into the kitchen area, she caught Randy watching her. He didn't look happy. That sense of being overprotected again made her frown. Her boss and her brother seemed to be made of the same cloth and it torqued her off. Now her hands shook for an entirely different reason.

Randy stepped out of the kitchen and headed in her direction. She turned and walked away from him before she said something that was not nice, or worse, yelled like she had something to be ashamed of. She had done nothing wrong by talking to the man so Randy had no reason to yell at her.

"Be right back!" she shouted to no one in particular. She needed to get some fresh air and calm down before she got herself in trouble for real.

Head down, she walked out the front door and circled the restaurant, intending to go inside through the back door the moment she cooled off.

Footsteps crunched on the gravel. Someone followed her and she darted a look over her shoulder to see who it was. The moment she recognized Kurt, she stopped. Her heart thumped, but it was more from *stray*, from fear of being followed -- and the shock of seeing him there -- than actual attraction. She'd fully expected to see Randy behind her, not Kurt.

"You miss me already, honey? Had to come and meet me outside?" He peered so intensely at her that her pulse started racing. His gaze slid to her mouth.

Her throat tightened and she couldn't seem to reply. "I--"

He stepped closer. "It's okay. I won't hurt you, honey."

A rush of adrenaline surged through her at his words. Georg had said the exact same thing the day they first met. Surely this man wouldn't be cruel like Georg had been. Nobody was that mean. But it was still weird to hear the same words come from this man's mouth.

"You're trembling. Are you okay?"

She shook her head to indicated no, still unable to speak.

"Here, wear my coat if it will help warm you up." He smiled and draped his jacket over her shoulders. He pulled it closed in the front, like swaddling a baby in a blanket. She had trouble breathing because he held on *too* tight.

"You scares me. Please, remove jacket. I am not cold."

His eyes widened as if in shock. He loosened his grip and removed his coat from her shoulders. "I scared you? Really? I'm sorry. Sometimes I don't realize how strong I am. You're so small and delicate. I hope I didn't hurt you too much."

Too much? She shook her head. She must be hearing him wrong.

"I am fine." She stated, staring at him and not sure what to say next, but not ready to leave his presence yet either. This man intrigued her in a way that she couldn't explain, or understand. That scared her most of all.

Tenderness filled his eyes as he touched her *litse*, her face. "You are very beautiful."

Heat scrambled over her skin, raising her awareness of him. She couldn't seem to look away even though he made her nervous by the way he peered so intensely at her, like he was going to *bakni,* to kiss her. She barely knew him, for goodness sake. But part of her wanted to kiss him, too, crazy as it seemed. Something deep inside her knew she'd like his kisses.

He closed his eyes and tipped his head down. She started to respond naturally, but had second thoughts and stepped back. She raised her arm to block him from getting closer. There was no way she would let him do that. Not yet, anyway. Not until she knew more about him. He could be married for all she knew. Her stomach rolled at the thought.

Kurt must've felt her hand heading toward his chest because he opened his eyes before his lips met hers. He frowned and studied her for a moment. After taking a long, slow breath, he said, "I'm sorry. I don't know what I was thinking. Forgive me for being so forward. It's just that you remind me so much of my wife who passed away several years ago. Sometimes I miss her and I lose my head. It won't happen again. Not unless you want it to."

She watched his mouth move and only caught about half of what he said. Something about a wife and about not thinking and losing his head. Or did he say she lost her head? It seemed like an apology of some kind even though it made no sense. Had his wife been beheaded by someone? "You are married?"

He shook his head, his eyes locked on hers. "No, ma'am. I'm a widower. Been one for a few years now."

"I am so sorry." She touched his arm and sought his gaze.

His eyes grew tender.

"Someone kill you wife?" Her hand slid down his arm to capture his fingers.

"What? No!" He released his hand from hers and crossed his arms. He seemed to search out everything around her, but wouldn't look her in the eyes. Maybe he was afraid he'd start crying because of grief. Better to let him down easy than hurt him unnecessarily. "Is okay. You need time for healing from losses. I understand this."

He nodded, his eyes captivating hers with intensity again. "Yes, but it helps to have someone to talk to about the pain."

"I listen to story, but not today. I must work." They stood for several long moments looking at each other; his attention fixed on her as if trying to read her thoughts. She heard a door open.

"Jovana, are you coming back? One of your tables is asking for their bill."

"I must go now." Without waiting for an answer, Jovana darted past him and ran back inside. She peered around and searched for the customers requesting their bill. A middle aged couple waved in her direction, but neither seemed very happy.

"I am so sorry. This is you bill." She handed it to the husband, but the woman snatched the paper from his hands. "I meet at register, please?"

Jovana smiled and walked over to the register as if she hadn't seen the way they fought. She waited as the couple argued quietly with each other. Finally the woman handed her a credit card and Jovana rang them up. The woman didn't include a tip on the receipt. A quick glance at the table told her that they had stiffed her completely.

With a heavy sigh she walked into the kitchen to compose herself. It had been a trying day. First, Kurt had shaken her up by getting too familiar, and then people who could obviously afford to leave her a good tip had stiffed her. What else could go wrong today?

Someone touched her shoulder and she stifled a scream with her hand. She'd been so deep in thought she hadn't noticed anyone behind her. She turned and scowled at Randy. "Do not touch. You scares me. Say words first."

"I didn't mean to startle you. So what did that guy want?" Randy frowned and watched her closely as if to gage her truthfulness.

She shrugged, unable to formulate the words to explain something she didn't understand herself.

"Jovana, I think you need to stay away from him. I don't have a good feeling about that guy."

The truth was she didn't either. But something about him still tugged at her heart. Something familiar and terrifying drew her and she had a difficult time resisting the pull. If she knew what it was that bothered her she might be able to handle it. But she didn't.

When Randy touched her arm, it felt entirely different. Almost painful, like the shock of a thousand needles poking her skin, or like lightening bolts zipping through her veins. And the genuine compassion and understanding in his eyes made her want to run fast in the other direction. He was too kind and she was undeserving of that kindness. He didn't know who she really was.

Jovana, you are saved by Grace. You are not who you once were.

She shivered in response to God comforting her with His undeniable truth.

"Please, just be careful." Randy's concerned gaze refused to leave hers.

The fear in his eyes made her stomach flip. She didn't know how to deal with him caring about her. It was hard enough resting secure in God's love, so when Randy showed the same fierce concern as her brother, it made her want to run screaming from him. She scowled harder. "Why you tell me this? Is not like you know this man is bad man."

"Sometimes you can just tell that about a person." He sighed. "Please, just think about it."

She watched him without agreeing for several long moments. Finally nodding her assent, she closed her eyes in a silent prayer. *God, give me wisdom and help me to not run from Your blessings.*

*****

Kurt sulked behind the wheel of his truck and went over every detail in his mind as he took a long drag from a cigarette. He'd tried to quit smoking several times, but it was no use, so he stopped trying. He'd been so sure she'd wanted him to kiss her until she pushed him away.

Lucky for her someone called and distracted him before he grabbed her and kissed her anyway. He had a feeling she would have been angry if he'd forced her to comply, just like his wife had been before he ended things between them on that fateful day. He shivered just thinking about how he'd had to dig her grave. It was such unpleasant work.

But Jovana was not his wife. She would respect him. He would make sure of that. First, he needed to win her trust. He had not accomplished that yet.

He had to play the game right or he'd lose her, plain and simple. He hated losing, and this time he'd almost lost control. He wanted her so badly he could taste the adrenaline pumping through his veins. It was too early in the game to take stupid chances like that again. He could not afford to mess things up. Not after he'd finally found the woman he'd been searching for.

So how was he to deal with the ache in his body when just being near her got him so worked up? He moaned just remembering the sensual look in her eyes. Timidity and curiosity merged in her gaze to tease his senses. Maybe he'd check out that stripper bar near the Fort. That would provide a little relief, at least for tonight.

He'd never had any trouble picking up a willing woman, thanks to his reasonably good looks. Yeah, when he'd gotten his fill, he'd be back to see Jovana.

This time he'd be smarter. He'd handle her better.

He'd tell her exactly what she wanted to hear.

Chapter Four

Randy thought about calling Bojan. He wanted to tell him about the strange customer who came to the restaurant just to watch his sister for hours at a time while she served other people, but he decided against it. Bojan would most likely overreact and Randy didn't want to do anything to make Jovana mistrust him. Not when he would be spending so much time with her in the near future. And that reality made him shiver with excitement every time he thought about it.

His cell phone vibrated in his pocket, pulling him from his thoughts. "Hello?"

"Is me, Bojan. I need favor, please."

"I'll see what I can do. What is it?"

"Laney in Tucson shopping for things last minute for wedding. I plan for to bring Jovana home for Laney but now I must go help Laney for flat tires. She cries and worry so I pick her up by Vail and call truck for towing. Can you do this?"

His boss has a tendency to confuse his sentence structure and tenses so badly that Randy often repeated what he thought Bojan said to see if he understood him correctly. "Are you saying that Laney is near Vail and needs a tow truck called, and because you are going to help her you won't be able to give Jovana a ride home?"

"Yes."

"I can do that. I'll come back and close up the restaurant after I bring her home so she won't have to wait around for me."

"Is good plan. *Blagodaram.*"

"You're welcome. Call me when you and Laney are back in town so I know you arrived okay."

"Is no problem. Bye."

Jovana had just entered the kitchen in time to hear the end of his conversation. The worried look on her face made Randy want to pull her into his arms and reassure her even though the situation with Laney and the flat tire really didn't call for it.

"Something wrong with Laney?"

He took a deep breath and exhaled slowly. "She has a flat in Vail. It's near Tucson. Bojan just called to tell me he was going to help her and wanted me to take you home after we close."

She glanced at the clock. "This is less than ten minutes."

"I can handle it. Don't you worry about a thing." Randy offered his most reassuring grin in hopes that if she saw he wasn't worried then she would follow suit. Instead, she looked at him like she thought he'd lost his mind. Her scrutiny made him self-consciously smooth his hair. His finger snagged on something.

A dried lump of sugar and dough from the sticky buns he had made fresh that morning had imbedded in his hair. The way she watched him made him want to cause a distraction, so he teased without thinking about how she might interpret it. "Just saving a snack for later."

The shocked look on her face was priceless.

"Just kidding." He laughed and tossed the dough into the trash.

"Wait! Do not move." She approached him with a serious expression and turned him around. She touched his hair and the sensation of her hands on his head heated him to the soles of his feet. The light scent of her shampoo wafted by and he sighed with pleasure. He felt a sudden tickling sensation and shuddered.

"You haves lice!" She squealed and jumped back.

Panic made Randy swat at his head and shiver. In fact, a girlish squeal erupted as he ruffled his hair before he realized what he was doing. "Ack! I thought something was making my head itch."

Jovana gave him an impish grin and chuckled behind her hand. After several seconds she hunched over and laughed with so much gusto he thought she'd start howling.

He squinted. Something fishy was going on. The mischievous look in her eyes made him pause.

"I cannot tell lies. Is joke." She snorted and as she laughed a few tears trickled down her face.

A chuckle erupted from him in response. She'd gotten him good with that one. "You stinker!"

Covering her mouth, she giggled some more. Then sadness crept into her eyes. She covered her forehead with her hand and bit her lip. Silent tears streamed down her face and she turned around so that her back faced him. Something was upsetting her, but what?

"You okay?" He reached for her shoulder and gently rested his hand there.

Her head shook briskly from side to side and she covered her face with her hands.

He wanted to touch her and provide some comfort, but it wouldn't be appropriate because she was his employee. So to help him keep a professional distance he gently squeezed her shoulder in reassurance and said, "Be right back."

Darting into the dining area he saw that the last customer had left the building. Several waitresses were clocking out. "See you tomorrow, Beth, Gina."

"Bye, Randy." Gina waved and Beth followed. Now the only people left in the diner were Randy, Jovana, and the dishwasher/cook Shep who had disappeared into the back of the building for a smoke, but had been gone for longer than it would take the average person to finish a cigarette.

Randy re-entered the kitchen and slipped past Jovana. She was wiping her face with a napkin. He peeked into the alley and found his employee talking to a seedy-looking character wearing a leather vest and a sleeveless tee. His arms were marked with spider web tattoos and other symbols. "You planning on coming back inside?"

"Sure." Shep gave the guy he was talking to a knuckle punch and ground his cigarette butt into the gravel. He headed toward Randy and stopped in front of him. "Need something?"

"I'm taking Jovana home. I'll be back in about a half hour. If I'm not back when it's time for you to leave make sure to lock up anyway, okay?" He tossed Shep the extra key.

"You got it." Shep whistled a tune from Snow White and the Seven Dwarfs as he grabbed a bucket full of dirty dishes. Without looking back, he started sorting the dishes and spraying them off.

Though Randy hated to suspect him just because he was an ex-con, he couldn't help wondering if the man could be trusted in the restaurant alone. Then again, the man was whistling a Disney tune, so maybe he wasn't dangerous. Randy always made sure he was the last one to leave the building. This would be the first time he'd leave the place in charge of someone else. Just to be safe, he walked into the dining area and locked the register. He slipped the key into his pocket.

Jovana stood by the front door wearing her jacket and shivering even though it wasn't cold outside. Her eyes seemed unfocused, like she was dwelling on a bad memory of some kind. She didn't look up until he waved his hand in front of her face.

"Want to tell me what that was all about?" He jerked his thumb toward the kitchen area.

"No." She glanced at her feet and waited until he pushed the door open and directed her outside.

Realizing it would be a bad idea to push her for information, he decided to pray for her instead as he opened the car door for her. Neither spoke as he drove her up the foothills to Laney's large house.

He parked on the driveway. When she didn't unclip her seatbelt he decided to turn off the engine. Maybe she was ready to talk now. He rested his sweaty hands on his knees and he turned to face her. A section of hair had fallen in her eyes. He moved it off her forehead, tucking the strands behind her ear. Something wonderful, like a honeysuckle scent, overwhelmed his senses. His pulse tripped as he inhaled and tried not to let the effect of her nearness show.

She scanned his eyes as if debating on whether to trust him or not. After several agonizing minutes she opened her mouth. "My ex-boyfriend, Georg, abuse me and leave me on streets for dead."

A sensation like ice water hitting him in the face made him gasp. He had not expected such a personal admission. Not sure what to say to that, he decided to be honest and tell her what he knew. "Bojan mentioned something like that to me. He didn't use those exact words, though. He just said you weren't ready for a boyfriend yet and that you had a bad experience in Macedonia."

"My *bratko* have no reasons to tell my problems to you." She squinted and looked like she was thinking hard on what to say next. Her teeth scraped her bottom lip.

He softened his voice so she would not be afraid. "He just worries about you getting hurt again. It's normal for a big brother to act that way."

"Maybe is normal for some, but is not okay for me. Is personal stuff he tells you?"

"No. Nothing personal. Just that you had a bad experience. That's all he said."

She squinted and searched his eyes skeptically. "You would tell me if I ask truth of you?"

He swallowed hard and nodded.

The tension in her eyes eased and her face softened.

"I don't want anyone hurting you either." He reached out to touch her face, but pulled back. He didn't want to be too forward. Things were already more intimate than they should be.

"You care for me be safe?"

His heart pounded painfully as he took in the hopeful look in her eyes. "Yes, of course."

"Good. I must go now." She unclipped her seatbelt and started to open her door.

In a flash he exited the vehicle and zipped around the front of the car. She was going to be treated right whether she wanted to be or not. He extended his hand to her.

Glancing up, she flashed him a bright smile. "When you do this I feel like queen."

"That's the idea." He couldn't help smiling back. My goodness but she was beautiful.

"I thank you for kindness." She allowed him to help her stand.

A warm bolt shot up his arm as he captured her gaze.

She sucked in a quick breath as if she'd felt it, too. He glanced at her lips and regretted it instantly. She'd caught him looking at her mouth, which now curved into a frown.

"Why you look at me this way?" She stared so intensely at him that he had to turn away.

Swallowing hard several times, he finally answered. "I'm sorry, but you're very beautiful."

"You sorry I beautiful?" She rolled her eyes. "Is strange phrase."

"Um..." He opened his mouth but wasn't sure how to reply.

Her brows rose as she watched for his reaction. The surprised expression on her face made him want to giggle like a girl. He never acted this stupid around women before, so why start now?

With a deep chuckle circling his words despite his effort to contain it, he answered, "I'm not sorry. I was just apologizing for staring at your mouth. I'll try to keep my eyes to myself."

She gasped. "What this mean? You haves glass eye?"

He rubbed his forehead and frowned. Where in the world did she get that idea? "No."

"Then how you take eye out?" She seemed genuinely stumped.

The moment he realized his blunder he laughed. "Oh, that's just an expression. That means I won't stare at you anymore if it makes you nervous."

A giggle burst from her lips. "You Americans make no sense with phrases. I will never learn these things. Is very hard. I see why Bojan have problem with Laney when they first meet."

"He did have difficulty for a while, but it obviously worked out."

"Yes, my *bratko* is happy. So is Laney. They are happy couple."

"It's hard to believe they are going to be married in a little over a week. Then they're off to Paris." He swallowed hard and regretted reminding her that they would be in the house alone.

She rubbed her arms. "I must go inside. Thank you for drive."

"You are very welcome. If you need anything just call me okay?" He walked her to the door.

"Okay." She started digging around in her purse. Then she patted down her pockets.

"Can't find your key?"

"I have in pocket. I check this when I leave house this morning."

"Maybe it fell out of your pocket. Let's check in my car."

She waited as he opened the door and then bent down to check under the seats. He had to look away because he appreciated the view of her shapely behind a bit too much. She squealed and jumped up. Her head connected with the door frame and a cracking sound made him wince.

"You okay?" Without thinking he grabbed her head and held it for a moment. The surprised look in her eyes made him let go.

Rubbing the back of her head, she lifted her other clasped hand to reveal a shiny silver key. She smiled and winced at the same time. "Yes. I find key."

Until he saw that expression, he wouldn't have thought it possible.

"I must haves hole in pocket." She giggled, still rubbing her head.

"You sure you're okay?" He moved out of the way so she could get past him. He closed the car door and followed her to the house. The memory of her silky hair between his fingers made his hands tingle. He wanted to touch her again.

She glanced over her shoulder. "Please, do not follow me."

He stopped cold. "Why not?'

"Man who abuse me, Georg, he follows me and this make me scared."

"He followed you?"

"Yes, he walk behind me and call me bad names and kick me if I not walk fast enough."

"What kind of man does something like that to a woman?"

She turned just enough to capture his gaze and said with a deadpan expression, "This man who say he loves me."

Without another word, she opened the door and slipped inside.

Ouch. That sad look on her face nearly did him in. His heart ached for her. At the same time he wondered why she'd looked him in the eyes when she'd told him that. Was she trying to warn him to stay away from her by disclosing that to him? He decided to ask Bojan about that later. For now he would take her statement at face value. She wanted him to know she'd been hurt by a man who claimed to love her once, and she wasn't risking it again. At least not with him.

But what about that guy at the restaurant? She seemed to sparkle whenever he spoke to her. A chill overtook him and he shuddered. Something about that man didn't feel right, but he couldn't prove anything yet. Regardless, he would protect Jovana at all costs.

Even if this time it cost him his life.

*****

Jovana watched Randy drive down the road and berated herself for bringing up Georg's abusive behavior. The less Randy knew about her former life, the better. If they were to be friends she wanted to start with a clean slate. Telling him about her former lover and her failed pregnancies would be a guaranteed turnoff. Then again, that might be the very disclosure that would keep her heart safe.

She decided then that was exactly what she'd do. If he tried anything with her she'd hit him with the heavy facts first. If that didn't work, she'd go into more detail. He'd certainly looked shocked enough from her admission about Georg's minor abuse, such as when he'd merely followed her and called her names. What would Randy think if he knew the full extent of Georg's abuse? Of the things he had forced her to do? No doubt he would find her repulsive.

The phone rang and Jovana paused. Should she answer the call or not? Her English was still pretty rough and when she got nervous she jumbled all three languages she spoke, so she made little sense even to herself.

She opted to let the phone go to the answering machine and listened closely.

"This is Kurt. Do I have the right house? I would like to speak to Jovana if she's there. Please have her call me any time day or night at 459-1111 when she gets this message. Thanks!"

Jovana stared at the phone and debated on what to do. She grabbed a pen and jotted the number onto a scrap sheet of paper she'd found in her purse. She listened to the message one more time to make sure she wrote the number down correctly, and then she deleted it. The last thing she needed was to have her big brother screening all of her friends, so the less he knew of Kurt, the better.

Reaching for the cordless phone fully intending to call Kurt back, she grabbed it on the first ring instead. She pushed the answer button. "Hello?"

"Jovana? It's Bojan." He spoke in his native language. "Laney is okay now so we'll be home soon. You must be ready for an early dinner. Laney and I wish to take you to nice place for eating, so wear a pretty dress, please."

"When will you be here?" Jovana glanced at her hair in the mirror and saw that it needed styling.

"In forty minutes. Can you wait by the front door?"

"I believe so. I'll take a quick shower first."

"Sounds good to me. See you soon, my dear *sestra*."

"Bye." Jovana stared at the phone for a moment and decided she could always call Kurt later. If she didn't hop in the shower within the next few minutes, her hair wouldn't have enough time to air dry.

With a sigh, she turned away from the answering machine and climbed the stairs. Kurt wasn't going anywhere, so she had nothing to worry about. She knew when a man was attracted to her. The one thing that bothered her, though, was how he'd gotten the phone number to the house. But obviously he cared enough to find out how to reach her, so she pushed the suspicion from her mind.

Giggling, she reflected on their conversation earlier that afternoon. She had a feeling if she returned his call right now Kurt would be at her doorstep in a heartbeat. He couldn't hide his obvious interest in her because she could see it in his eyes. Maybe he wanted her to know that he liked her. She didn't mind, though, because she *isto taka,* she liked him also.

When she reached the top of the stairs she closed her eyes for a moment and remembered the rush she'd felt when Kurt had looked like he wanted to kiss her. Smiling, she imagined him following through this time. Warmth filled her as she reveled in the sensation of being wanted by a man again.

She reached into her purse and checked her wallet to make sure the paper with his phone number on it was still there. She didn't want to lose the number like she had almost lost the house key.

After everyone went to bed, she would call Kurt back. He had said any time, hadn't he? Even midnight? When it seemed safe enough to call him without Bojan finding out, she would see if he'd really meant what he'd said.

And if luck had her way, she would arrange to see him without getting caught.

Chapter Five

Randy debated whether or not to tell Bojan about his concerns. The fine line between helping and hurting in this case made him pray for discernment. He wanted to protect Jovana, but he didn't want to hurt her feelings in the process. She was obviously very sensitive about people supervising her behavior like she was still a child. He didn't blame her for resenting that, but she also didn't know how vulnerable she was to abuse because she was unfamiliar with the American culture.

He'd originally suspected she had not been intimate with a man, but that was before she implied some things about Georg and the way he had treated her. Maybe he'd sexually abused her, too. The thought made him cringe. He didn't want to remind Jovana of her past experiences with Georg. What kind of scumbag pushed his girlfriend and kicked her for not walking fast enough?

Pulling his cell phone from the clip on his belt, he started to dial Bojan's number. His phone vibrated in the middle of his dialing. How weird that they'd thought to call each other at the same time.

"*Alo?*"

"*Kade ti?*" Where are you?

"*Vo moj kola.*" In my car.

"*Tebe zafaten?*' You busy?

The phrases were getting harder to decipher so he continued in English. "Not really."

"Good, meet at new Greek restaurant in town."

Randy's heart squeezed and his muscles stiffened from head to toe. He hadn't eaten Greek food since the night of the attack. Bile rose in his throat and he swallowed the bitterness. "I don't think I can, boss. It's too hard for me to relive that stuff."

"How must you come over *stravs* if you not try this?"

"I'm sorry, Boss, but I'll have to pass this time. I'm not ready yet." He rubbed his forehead, hating that terror still struck his heart at the mere mention of Greek food. Even though the new restaurant in town was a chain and not privately owned, the scent alone might make him nauseous. The sound of crashing dishes and an *Opa* might set him off, too. He couldn't risk it.

"I bring Jovana to this place for dinner at restaurant. She comes tonight."

"Are you saying Jovana will be there?" He swallowed hard. He'd hate to miss a chance to spend time with her. Especially if that meant she'd feel safer with him when he stayed with her.

"Yes, I say this. You will change mind, please?"

"Who else will be there?"

"Laney and Jovana is only womens. Then is you and me. Is okay for you?"

It was more than okay. His heart melted at the idea of sitting near Jovana and sharing a meal together even if his boss and fiancée were present the entire time. He exhaled loudly and tried to force the fear from his chest. "Okay, I'll go."

"Is good. I pay for food. You must see Jovana to know her for trust."

"When do you want me to meet you?"

"Twenty minutes. *Fala!*"

"*Molam*." Randy pressed the off button and set the phone on the seat beside him. He made a U turn at the next cement island and headed in the direction of the new restaurant, sweating the entire way.

After parking, he prayed for peace as he stared at the entrance and took several deep breaths. He could do this, he told himself as he slowly entered the building. The scent of roasted lamb made his mouth water and his stomach rebel at the same time. How he wished Bojan had selected another place to eat, but since he was already in the building he tried his best to remain calm. No doubt Jovana would love to eat Greek food if it gave her pleasant memories. Then again, it might upset her if it reminded her of that creep Georg.

He informed the hostess that he was meeting friends and to please direct them to his table when they arrived. Then he waited. And waited. His mind wandered to that fateful night as a familiar Greek song played in the background. The volume grew louder and the staff started their traditional dance, which ended with a crashing plate. He winced and sucked in his breath as he tried to calm his racing pulse. Tears blurred his vision and he forced his eyes shut.

Get a grip, Randy. You're in a public place.

But voices from the past clamored in his head.

"Back up now! That's it. Now put your hands over your head."

"Hey, look what I found here."

Frightened whimpers told him they'd found Melody in the back room. Her eyes pleaded with him to save her. He debated on what to do and lowered his hands. "Don't touch her!"

He felt a gust of air behind his skull and heard a crack. Then everything went black.

A lump formed in his throat and he brushed the tears from his lashes. He would hold it together tonight if it killed him. What happened was in the past. Bojan was right. He needed to put the fear behind him. But the muffled sound of Melody's pleas for help still rang in the back of his head. That sense of helplessness tore over him again and he started to tremble.

"Please, God, heal me from my memories of that night," he whispered and closed his eyes again. When he felt his muscles finally relaxing, he opened his eyes and searched the area, but no one had arrived yet. Staring out the window, he blocked his mind from allowing further memories to invade his peace until he finally saw Bojan's yellow Hummer approach and park next to his vehicle. He watched through the restaurant's bay window as Bojan helped the ladies exit the car. They headed toward the restaurant as a group.

His jaw dropped. Jovana looked smoking hot in a black dress and fluffy shawl. The dress seemed a bit too long, but she had a belt cinched around her waist so it fit her curves nicely. He smiled as he took in her gorgeous hair. It hung over her shawl and shoulders like a satin mantle. She looked so feminine and innocent as she walked along, her bright smile almost naïve enough to make him think she was just a high school student. How much of the real world had touched her life? Certainly more than he'd originally thought given her comments about that sicko Georg. A vision from that night in Tucson flashed before his eyes, but he forced the memory away.

Hopefully Jovana hadn't been raped. He knew what that could do to damage a young woman's soul. He'd seen the lasting effect on Melody and didn't know if he could handle the continual rejection that often came with such pain. No doubt Melody suffered from ongoing fear because the last he'd heard she was still in therapy to deal with the trauma.

He stood and left the table to greet them but caught sight of someone in the parking lot from the corner of his eye. That same middle-aged man from *The Diner* had parked several rows over and stepped out of his car to follow them. He lit a cigarette as he watched them enter the restaurant. Once they were inside, instead of coming in to get a table he ground out his cigarette and went back to his vehicle. But he didn't start his car and drive away. How strange.

"Boki, you not tell me Ron-dee meet here for dinner."

Was that irritation in her voice? Not good.

Randy stood and extended his hand. "It's good to see you, too, Jovana."

She frowned half-heartedly and received his offered hand.

Even that pout looked sexy. Lord help him.

"Is okay for you here. Boki just not say this to me, so is surprise. That is all."

Randy glanced at his boss, who shrugged.

She shot Bojan a scowl and said something he didn't understand, but it sounded like Greek and not Macedonian. Her brother replied and they went back and forth for a minute.

Laney tapped Bojan's arm. "Stop talking if you can't argue in English. I feel left out."

"I tell my *sestra* that I want you come eat and did not want you to refuse so I not say this. I am sorry." Bojan drooped his lip and widened his eyes, which caused Jovana to laugh and hit his arm.

"My crazy *bratko*." Jovana squealed. "You so bad!"

Laney giggled. "I can't resist him when he does that either." She looped her arm in her fiancé's and chose a seat. Bojan arranged the chair for her and set her items on the extra seat at the table.

Randy pulled out a chair for Jovana, too, and he helped her with her purse and shawl. From where he stood he could see down the front of her dress, which had a low neck and hung loosely over her small, but shapely breasts. He couldn't help noticing she hadn't worn a bra either.

Lord, help him keep his eyes in a proper place. This was going to be a challenging evening. So far his eyes wanted to rivet to the front of her dress and enjoy that hint of cleavage exposed by the drooping neckline. He had to force himself to keep his attention on her face. Women had no idea how hard it was for men to behave when they wore such attractive clothing, especially when it was just cool enough outside to make her braless chest super obvious. Man, and that was his greatest weakness, too. He groaned and closed his eyes for a moment as he prayed for self-control.

When he opened his eyes he saw the hint of a smile on Bojan's face, like he'd noticed Randy's suffering and found it amusing. If the man wasn't his boss he'd walk out right now. It ruffled Randy that Bojan seemed to enjoy seeing his discomfort. Just because he was getting married soon and would get some relief from the waiting game didn't mean he should tease Randy about his unmet needs.

Randy frowned at Bojan. His boss seemed to catch the meaning in his gesture and cleared his throat. Randy shot a quick glance at Jovana. She'd obviously noticed his silent communication with her brother because that sad expression had returned to her eyes. He wished he hadn't been the cause, but knew in his gut that somehow he had made her sad. She probably thought he was not happy to be there with her. Oh, if she only knew how happy it actually made him.

The waiter came to their table to get their drink orders. He smiled at Jovana a little too long in Randy's opinion, but she didn't seem to notice. Jovana smiled and said in heavily accented English, "I like water with lemon slice, please, and one glass of Merlot."

After they all nodded their agreement that they too wanted wine, the waiter left. Randy couldn't help noticing how her accent was stronger when speaking to strangers. Maybe it was nerves. So did that mean that she was comfortable around him because her accent was less noticeable? He could only hope that was true.

Glancing at her, he wanted to make light conversation but wasn't sure what to say. The necklace she wore sparkled and his attention dropped lower. Oh my, he could see that she was still a bit cold. He wanted to cover her up before his eyes glazed over and locked on her upper torso, so he grabbed her shawl and blurted, "Would you like this back?"

Her brows knit in apparent confusion. "I am fine, thank you."

Still staring as he laid the shawl on the seat beside him, he muttered, "If you're sure..."

She'd noticed his attention on her chest. "What you look to see?"

The waiter returned and placed their drinks in front of them, giving him a chance to come up with an acceptable answer. Clearing his throat, he gestured toward his neck and then he pointed at hers. "That's a nice necklace."

Her face lit up and she touched it. "Laney gives me this for wedding. It is beautiful, is it not?"

A pathetic sigh escaped from him before he could stop it. "Yes, very beautiful."

Bojan hid his laugh with a cough and started choking on his water. Laney slapped his back. "You okay? Did you inhale your water?"

He nodded and smiled as he settled down and took another sip.

Randy didn't find the situation amusing at all. He was just about to say something when Jovana finished a long drink with a pretty little sigh. He nearly lost it when her eyes closed for a moment and imagined kissing those moist lips. They put Jolie's to shame.

She set her glass on the table and Randy shifted uncomfortably in his seat. Drat that pulsing response his body seemed to have from her every move. She was too sexy for her own good.

"Mmm... is very... how you say, yummy?"

"Your water is yummy?" He grinned and tried to shrug off the power she had over his emotions.

"Yes." Her mouth glistened and he felt his body growing more tense and frustrated by the moment. He found it hard enough not to stare at her when she wore that cheesy waitress uniform at work. But seeing her in that silk dress and having her sitting so close that he could almost feel her moist lips on his was downright cruel. How in the world was he going to be in the same house with this woman for two weeks without going mad from wanting what he so obviously could not have?

"God, we thank for food and for Randy and Jovana eat dinner for me and Laney to share. Bless everyone at table and protect from harm. Amen."

Randy had been so fixated on Jovana's moist lips that he found it hard to close his eyes and join in the blessing for the food. He groaned inwardly and kept his eyes closed after the prayer ended. He begged God to give him self-control. He was typically one of the most self-controlled men he knew and yet he struggled big time right now.

Looking at pictures of scantily clad women rarely tempted him, but put a live woman with sex appeal and a hot accent next to him and his willpower turned to mush. She was driving him crazy. That was why he'd always avoided dating. He refused to toy with things he was not able to keep, like a wife. So unless he planned to marry Jovana someday, he needed to remember that.

"What you think, Ron-dee?"

"Huh?" He totally missed the question and wasn't quite sure how to explain why. So he didn't.

"You not want for listen to me?" She pouted playfully and captured his gaze once again.

"Oh, I could listen to you for hours," he muttered.

"What you say?"

"Nothing important. My mind just drifted. It happens." He grinned. "Sorry."

She grinned back and the delight in her eyes overcame the sadness. "Must I repeat question?"

"Please do." He rested his chin on his fist and leaned on the table with his elbow. Not the best table manners, but at least she knew that she had his undivided attention now.

Blushing, she said, "Now I not want to tell you what I say."

"Why not?" He sat up straight.

"You make me... how you say... nervous?" She blinked and the color in her cheeks bloomed.

"I do? Why?" He rubbed his wet palms on his slacks. If anyone was nervous here, it was him.

"You stare at me." She squinted and then sniffed. "I do not like men stare."

The way she said it irritated him. "It doesn't seem to bother you when that man at the restaurant stares at you. In fact, you flirt right back with him." That was a stupid, jealous thing to say, but it was too late to take it back. Now he felt like an idiot.

Her lips pressed together and she turned her face away, no doubt blinking back tears. Bojan and Laney stared at him as if in shock that he would say something like that. Uh oh.

He touched Jovana's arm. "I'm sorry, that was uncalled for."

"Do not touch me," she hissed and moved her arm, her face still turned away. She bowed her head for a moment, pulled in a deep breath, then reached for her wine glass. She exhaled slowly and took a long drink. He could swear there were tears clinging to her lashes. Peering at him from the corner of her eye, she tipped her head back and downed the rest.

Was this God's way of answering his prayer to help him resist temptation? Since she was obviously angry with him right now his libido had cooled and his self-control had returned. Truth was he realized it probably wasn't God's doing. It was his own stupid flesh getting him into trouble with her.

Bojan leaned forward on the table and grumped, "You haves man flirt with you at diner?"

His deep, stern tone made Randy glance over at Jovana. Now he understood why she didn't want her brother to know her business. He looked ready to kill whoever dared to hit on his sister.

"Maybe I exaggerated a bit." Randy rested his hand on Bojan's for a split second to get his attention. "I'm just acting stupid. Ignore me, okay?"

Jovana glanced at Randy from the corner of her eye and he saw relief reflected there. He tried to communicate his apology with his eyes and hoped she would forgive him. She tipped her head down and folded her hands on her lap.

"Is this true, my *sestra*? Is man who flirts with you at diner?"

She bit her lower lip and hesitated. "I do not know of such a man."

Bojan stared at her for a minute, and then glanced at Randy, who feigned innocence and shrugged. He prayed Bojan would believe him.

Laney cleared her throat. Their waiter had returned to take their orders and slipped another glass of wine in front of Jovana since her glass was now empty. Randy wondered if all Europeans drank their wine so quickly. He rarely had wine with a meal, but when he did have some he made sure to savor it.

After the waiter took their orders he mentally kicked himself for drawing attention to Jovana and possibly incurring her brother's wrath. She probably had no idea who Randy referred to. In fact, she was probably oblivious of the man's attentions and it was all in his head. He glanced out the window to see if the man still waited outside, but his car was now gone.

Maybe Randy's mind was playing tricks on him again. He reached under his vest and patted his gun to make sure it was still here. He always packed it just in case. He had all the protection a man needed packed in his 9MM. He looked up and caught Laney, Bojan and Jovana watching him. They must've seen him checking for his gun and wondered what he was thinking. He'd also noticed his cell phone had gone missing from his belt clip and decided to ease their minds.

"Just checking for my phone. I think I left it in my car."

Jovana's shoulders seemed to relax after his comment, but she still stared at his holster with wide eyes. She had obviously noticed he carried a gun. He couldn't help wondering if Georg had ever used one to intimidate her.

He had a sinking feeling that there were things about Georg that if he knew the details they would make him angry enough to shoot the man. What if guns made her nervous? He didn't know what he'd do. He didn't want to resemble Georg in any way, but if she asked him to leave his gun at home, he didn't know if he could do that. Not even for her.

*****

Kurt decided not to wait on Jovana. She was sitting at the table with two men and another woman, so she had to be on a double date. He didn't want to scare her by pouncing on her the moment they left the restaurant, so he decided to go back home and wait. No doubt their time at the restaurant would drag on for her since she really wanted to be with him. He could sense that whenever she looked at him. She didn't want to date the manager of *The Diner*, and he wished he could intervene and save her from a boring evening.

With one last glance at the restaurant, he decided to sabotage the young manager's plans tonight. He recognized the guy's car. Most likely Jovana would leave with the people who brought her. So if the other man intended to follow them after dinner, he'd make it difficult for him.

He reached inside his pocket and yanked out his Leatherman. Pulling out the corkscrew, he slammed the sharp tip into the restaurant manager's tire and pushed until he heard it hiss. Then he extracted and folded the tool and slipped it back into his pocket. He stepped over to his car and hoped nobody had seen him jacking her blind date's tire.

She would call him tonight and he would be ready for her. She didn't look happy with her company, so his gut told him that she'd been set up and wasn't enjoying herself. He'd make sure to fix that when she called him later. Thankfully one of her coworkers had told him the name of the woman she lived with or he wouldn't have been able to leave her a message in the first place.

Yeah, she'd enjoy herself with him. That sexy little black dress made her difficult to resist, but he'd wait if he must. They'd have a great time later. He'd make sure of it.

*****

"You sure is okay for you do this?" Bojan's eyes pleaded for a positive response.

Bojan and Laney would never get to the play at the theater in time if they dropped Jovana off at home first, so he'd designated Randy to be her chauffeur. He seemed a bit worried that his sister was swaying on her feet, so Randy wanted to put his mind at ease.

"I'll take good care of her. She's safe with me." Randy smiled even though his stomach tensed at the idea of being alone in his car with Jovana, especially since she'd had a bit too much to drink. But he'd have to get used to being alone with her sooner or later if he was going to drive her to work and back every day once Bojan and Laney left for Paris.

"Many thanks, friend. My *sestra* is not good for drinking. I not want her to do this."

"She's an adult. You can't protect her from everything." He peered at her and could see why Bojan was concerned. She looked so young and vulnerable as she leaned against him.

Jovana's eyelids drooped and she swayed on her feet. "I not have drink *tsrveno vino* for year."

Randy steadied her with his arm wrapped around her shoulders. "I can see that."

"I am sorry for too much drink." She yawned and leaned against him. "Georg is drunk."

Such a large glass would easily make a small woman sway on her feet and she'd had two glasses. Jovana hadn't eaten much to go with her wine so it wouldn't surprise him if she was actually drunk. He'd had a large glass, too, but he was close to one hundred and ninety pounds and had eaten plenty, so most of the effect had already worn off.

She snuggled close and wrapped her hands around his bicep, her cheek resting against his arm as she sighed. Bojan raised his brows and Randy gave him a reassuring nod. "We'll be fine."

"She is still baby Christian. You must be strong."

He swallowed hard. "Not a problem."

"I no baby, Boki," she muttered against Randy's shirt.

Bojan nodded and left the building with Laney. Randy heard Laney say, "You have to trust him if we're going to leave them together while we're gone."

Randy took the comment to heart. He guided Jovana to the door and was careful with her so she wouldn't stumble. She felt like a small bird under his arm, and like a mother hen, a fierce sense of protectiveness came over him. What kind of monster had this Georg guy been anyway? And what did she mean by Georg is drunk?

He opened the door and held it for her. She stepped into the cool night air and shivered violently. "Is cold!"

Her shawl slipped off one shoulder and her dress strap followed, exposing her bare shoulder. She broke away from him and fought with the dress to get it back up, but lost her footing. He grabbed her before she fell from the step and twisted her ankle. She relaxed against him and giggled, inhaling deeply. "Mmmm... You smell like Georg."

He stiffened. From what he knew of the man, that couldn't be good. Or could it? He needed to know more about the guy before he could decide if he'd just been insulted or given a high compliment.

"And what does that smell like? Wine?" he asked as he directed her to the car.

She stopped and glanced up at him with a seductive look in her eyes. "Like sexy man."

Okay, that was a mixed message if he'd ever gotten one. She'd been hurt by the guy and yet she thought he was sexy. Women could be so confusing. He remembered that from growing up with his older sister and listening to her friends talk about boys.

He was about to start walking again when she asked, "Hold me, please?"

"I don't think that's a good idea." He pulled away from her.

"But is very cold." Her voice sounded pouty. "Please?"

One glance at the front of her dress confirmed her words and heated him to the core. His biggest weakness of the flesh -- her breasts -- were mere inches from him. He had to fight the urge to pull her against him and kiss her with such passion that they would burn from the heat they created.

She pressed against him and kissed his shirt. "I want some *baknuva*, baby."

He groaned. The idea of kissing her at any time was a huge turn-on, but he couldn't give in to his desire. Not when she was lit like this. "You're drunk, Jovana. I won't take advantage of you."

Tilting her face toward his, she traced his lip with her nail and asked huskily, "But is no problem if I want this, yes? You like?"

Of course he knew what *baknuva* meant. Sure he'd love that. He was a man. And though he loved Jesus and had saved himself, he might not be able to stop if she wanted more. Right now he wasn't sure how else to control the situation except by keeping his hands to himself. No doubt his expression spoke volumes because she sniffed her unhappiness.

"Do you not want me, Ron-dee?" she asked in Macedonian as she once again touched his lower lip. Her thumb started stroking it while she gazed at him with a hungry look in her eyes.

At least she meant him and not that creep Georg this time. He opened his mouth but all the words were locked in his mind and he couldn't pull them out. He could only stare into her eyes. His lips were on fire and other parts of him started throbbing painfully. He needed to get away, and fast.

She stepped back a few feet and gestured at her body, her legs still off balance. "You not want me? Is it not good to love me like this?" She raked her lip with her teeth and lunged for his collar.

"I didn't say... that." Randy forced himself to look away. He turned her around and started guiding her to the car, making sure to have as little contact as possible. He didn't trust his hands.

"Why do you not like me?" Jovana stopped and yanked his sleeve.

"I didn't say that." Sheesh, now he was repeating himself. He gently propelled her forward.

She glanced over her shoulder. "You do like me?"

"Of course I like you. I'm not like Georg. I know how to respect a woman."

Her body went limp and she started to cry. Drat that impulsive mouth of his.

"I'm sorry." He turned her until she faced him. He touched her cheek as he spoke softly, "I'm sorry. I didn't mean to make you cry."

"Georg, he evil man. He rape me. His friends rape me. I hate them." She growled, and started crying all over again. Her shoulders hunched as she leaned her forehead against his chest.

His friends had raped her? It was bad enough that Georg would do that to his girlfriend, but to have his friends join him? What kind of sick person did that? "Has Georg been arrested?"

Jovana stepped back and looked at him like he'd just said the dumbest thing. "No. But is okay."

"What? How is that okay?" She made no sense at all.

She shrugged and looked to the side, avoiding eye contact. "He cannot hurt me in America. I do not know if Georg lives or dies. I do not care."

Grabbing her shoulders, he pulled her to him to comfort her. Then again, he needed to comfort himself. The information she'd just given him disturbed him beyond anything he'd heard thus far. In fact, this new revelation of hers was even more disgusting than what had happened to Melody. He wanted Jovana to understand his heartfelt concern, so he held her face and peered into her eyes. "I understand. I'm sorry they hurt you."

She frowned and turned her face away. "You understand nothing."

Dropping his hands in stunned response, he resisted the urge to punch the side of his car. After counting for twenty seconds and inhaling slowly, he regained his composure. He opened the car door and removed his cell phone from the seat before getting her settled. After starting the engine, he pulled out of his parking space and heard a bump, bump, bump sound. Stifling an angry reaction so he wouldn't scare her, he pulled over. "I need to change the tire."

She didn't answer, but stared out the window, unblinking.

"This is going to take awhile."

Closing her eyes, she lay back in the seat. Within minutes he heard a light snoring sound. She'd crashed in the car. Maybe when she woke she'd be in better spirits.

Almost thirty minutes later he'd finished changing the tire and climbed back inside. Jovana was still sleeping, but her skin felt cold. Too cold.

A stream of drool connected her lip to her shirt. Just a few degrees cooler and it would've turned into an icicle. He couldn't remember the last time it was this cool in the fall. He started the engine and cranked up the heater to warm her before they arrived at Laney's house. It seemed to work as she began stirring by the time he was halfway up the road ten minutes later.

"Is hot in *kola*."

With a sheepish grin, he glanced at her. "You were cold and drooling. I had to warm you up."

A sly grin tugged at her lips and she said in a rough voice. "Is more fun ways to warm up than for heat from *kola* burn skin."

He reached under the dash and felt her shin. Her skin was so hot he shut off the heater. "Sorry!"

She waved her hand as if to brush off the apology. "Tell me. What is drool?"

A chuckle escaped him. "It's spit. You know, slobber?"

She grunted and unclipped her seatbelt without responding. It was as if she'd never heard him. He watched as she pulled her legs to her chest and rested her cheek on her knees. In an instant she'd fallen back asleep.

He pulled up in front of Laney's house and the floodlight came on. Not sure what to do next, he gently tapped her knee. "Jovana. Pssst! We're home."

Her lips moved slightly but she didn't stir. She was out cold again. He got out of his car and walked around to her door. He leaned inside and spoke louder this time. "I said we're home."

Jovana's eyes flew open and she screamed, raising the hair on the back of his neck. He dodged away from her so she couldn't hit him. After flailing a moment, she tucked her head between her knees and covered her skull with her arms. She cried and said words in her native tongue that he didn't understand, but her tone told him she was terrified of whoever she thought he was.

Probably Georg. He muttered under his breath, "You sick bast--jerk!"

His eyes stung and he clenched his fists, wanting to kill the animal and apologize to the Lord for his vicious thoughts at the same time. He swiped a tear from his cheek and took a deep breath. She needed to feel safe. If she heard him cussing about her ex he wouldn't accomplish that.

He spoke gently and touched her arm hoping that would show her that he was not that monster or someone she should fear. "It's me, Jovana. It's Randy."

Peering up at him with wet, bloodshot eyes, she squeaked out, "Ron-dee?"

"Yes, it's me. I'm just bringing you home. You've had too much to drink."

She blinked several times and collected herself. "I okay now."

He offered his hand and helped her out of the car. When her dress slipped from her shoulder again he hesitated, but carefully moved the strap back into place. His thumb stroked her shoulder, unable to resist touching her creamy skin.

Jovana glanced up and watched him for several long seconds. She bit her lip and stared at his mouth. Everything stilled around them as she licked her lips and reached for the back of his head. Her fingers plunged into his hair and massaged his skull.

It felt so heavenly, he groaned.

"I trust you, Ron-dee." Her large brown eyes begged him to kiss her.

Before he could respond, sudden piercing barks erupted from inside the house. Jovana laughed and jerked away from him. "Is Dude and Baby happy for seeing me."

The spell had broken, and though disappointed, he sighed with relief. He wouldn't have been able to resist her if she'd tried to kiss him, drunk or not. "Goodnight, Jovana."

She turned and stumbled slightly, but righted herself. Searching through her purse for several minutes, she finally produced the house key. "Many thanks for drive."

"Any time." He watched as she unlocked the door and was immediately pounced on by two frantic Chihuahuas. She crouched down to pet them and receive their tiny kisses on her cheeks. A wave of her hand told him she felt good enough to take things from there.

With a heavy sigh he turned and re-entered his car. Thanking God that he hadn't done anything he'd regret later, he started driving back down the mountain. So many things had happened between them he didn't know which event to savor first. But then he remembered he had no business savoring anything. She had only flirted with him because she'd had too much to drink. She wouldn't want him when she was sober.

If he hadn't had Christian convictions he could've taken whatever he'd wanted from her. But he did have convictions, so he vowed he would protect her.

Even if he had to protect her from himself.

Chapter Six

Jovana laughed at the *kuchinja*, those cute little dogs, who continued licking her face with fervor after she closed the door and waved at Randy to leave. She soon tired of them but still felt tipsy enough that she couldn't seem to move from the floor. She barely remembered the drive to her house.

Not long after Georg introduced her to alcohol, she'd started having blackouts because she couldn't handle the effect alcohol had on her system. No doubt she'd made a *budala*, a fool of herself in front of Randy. She cringed when she thought about what she might have done.

She thought a few drinks would help her relax around him, but instead the alcohol seemed to have brought out the old Jovana, the one that had been put to death when she found her new life in Christ. Memories from that horrible time made bile crawl up her throat. In the past she'd used alcohol to deaden the pain from living with an abusive man. Just one glass brought that all back, and two glasses made her nearly black out. She cringed to think of what she may have said or done with her boss. Hopefully she hadn't propositioned him for sex, which was something Georg had trained her to do to avoid a beating and to acquire drugs to fill his insatiable appetite.

But try as she might, she couldn't remember a thing from the past hour. However, the memories from her past life with Georg wouldn't leave. If only she could erase them. Blot them out forever.

When Georg had forced her to proposition men for money to buy drugs she'd obeyed out of a desperate attempt to survive. If she thought too long about those days she'd feel dirty -- like the woman caught in adultery -- so she suppressed the memories. But every now and then they would still come back to taunt her. Being the honorable man Randy was, she knew he wouldn't take her up on anything she'd offered, but that didn't lessen the embarrassment she'd feel if she found out she'd acted that way with him. Hopefully he wouldn't bring it up because the humiliation would be unbearable.

Vowing to never take another drink, she confessed to the Lord what she'd done even though she didn't remember a thing. She promised to live for Christ and not repeat any part of her sick past.

Once she finished meditating she stood to go to the kitchen and make some coffee, but her heel caught on the hem of her dress. She hit the ceramic tile floor.

Hard.

Her kneecap throbbed and she started to cry. Not just from the pain her body felt, but from the memories of her former life. As she lay on the tile and sobbed, she examined the flesh around her knee. No doubt she'd have a bruise by morning. She rubbed the tender area, trying to stand and at the same time untangle the heel that snagged on the material, but she failed miserably. The fact that her head spun and her body was still weak from too much to drink didn't help her situation.

The phone at the bottom of the stairs rang and she again fought to stand without ripping the material. The dogs yipped and yapped all around her and the noise hurt her ears, so she shoved them aside. She could hear Kurt talking into the machine and asking where she was and to please call him.

In desperation she kicked the tangled up shoe from her foot. A ripping sound told her she'd ruined the borrowed dress. She limped over to the phone while leaning against the wall with one hand for support. A dial tone sounded. She'd missed his call.

Staring at the phone for several minutes, she debated what to do next. Reaching for her purse, she found no wallet inside. Panic rose in her throat. Her green card and money were in her wallet. She had to find it or she would be sent back to Macedonia where she could run into Georg!

Glancing at the door, she swallowed hard and searched the area while crawling on her knees on the hard floor. She slipped into the garage, but didn't see her wallet anywhere. She groaned and wept until she realized that it probably fell out in his *kola*, his car and he would give it back to her tomorrow at work. But how was she supposed to get Kurt's number to call him back if the number was in her wallet? He hadn't left his number this time when he left his message. Or had he? She pressed the replay button and listened.

"Jovana, honey, I need you to call me back. I have something to give you. It's a surprise, but I think you'll like it. Please call me tonight when you get back from dinner. I'll be waiting to hear from you, beautiful."

No mention of his number. He probably thought she'd written it down from the last message he'd left. She had, but it didn't do her any good if she couldn't find it. Grunting her disgust, she pushed the erase button so Laney wouldn't get the message.

After she'd erased the message she reflected on what Kurt said. How did he know she'd gone to a restaurant tonight? Or was she remembering things wrong? Oh, she hated how her brain felt all muzzy inside and stupid from the wine. She could hardly think, so it was probably best she didn't call Kurt back right now. She'd probably revert to the old Jovana and offer to sleep with him. That would be the worst thing she could do.

Her mouth felt dank and a bit dry so she stumbled toward the kitchen for water and realized when she was halfway there that tossing off the other shoe would help her walk without her legs jerking around. The dogs nipped at her feet and hadn't stopped despite her continual movement. Her frustration grew from the constant barking and she held her hands over her ears. "Ahhh! Quiet!"

Babe and Dude paused for a moment, but then resumed their frenzied yipping.

"Go!" Jovana pointed at the stairs and the *kuchinja* started running up the steps. Though loud and annoying when they were excited, at least they obeyed when they were told to do something. If only she would do the same with God, her life would be less complicated. Bojan seemed to have no trouble hearing God's voice and doing His bidding, but she didn't feel the same closeness that she had when she first found the Lord.

Whenever she asked him how he stayed close to Jesus, Bojan told her it was from reading God's Word, the Bible, that helped him know God's peace. But she didn't understand how doing that would make a difference in her life. She hadn't done much reading of the Scriptures even though she'd had a Macedonian translation at her *baba's*. Plus, her brother had one she could borrow, so she had no excuse to be lazy.

She knelt on the floor and bowed her head as she prayed once more in her native tongue. "Please God. Forgive me for drinking too much and help me to start tomorrow like a new person."

Tears of repentance flowed until they dried up and she had none left to offer. Sleep overtook her and she slipped into a dreamless state. The next thing she knew someone was shaking her.

"Wake up!" Someone tapped her cheek as she forced her eyes open.

Bojan and Laney crouched over her. Her brother's eyes flamed with anger and he yelled in Macedonian, "Who did this? Tell me now or I'll beat truth from Randy and fire him."

"Did what?" Her voice sounded hoarse and her lips were dry. She needed some lip balm to moisten them. Her tongue felt swollen in her mouth. No doubt she looked a mess. She glanced around her, confused. Why was she lying on the kitchen tile?

"You have a bruise on your leg and black eyes. Somehow your dress was torn and I found you lying on the floor unconscious."

She glanced around at her pathetic state and had to agree it must look *losho,* bad to them. No doubt the black eyes were from the mascara smudged on her face. Or lack of sleep. She spoke to Bojan in Macedonian and hoped she reported the facts correctly. "I don't remember. I think I tripped and fell on my way to the kitchen. I must have caught the dress in my shoe and... that's all I remember."

"Did Randy hurt you? Tell me the truth." His scowl made her shrink back.

"No." She shook her head vehemently so he would see Randy was no threat.

"You must tell me truth." He grabbed her arms and held her tight so she had to look at him.

"He brought me to the door and I let myself inside. I told him to go home and he drove off." At least that's what she assumed happened based on the sketchy memories she managed to retain. Since she couldn't remember the exact details, she didn't really know the truth.

Bojan released her. "Good. He must not have known you would hurt yourself or he would never have left you on the floor. Or maybe he was worried because you were drunk and he didn't want it to look bad if he stayed here with you like this."

She blinked. "Maybe. I think so."

He reverted back to English. "Laney please help *sestra* up steps for bedroom."

Laney glanced at Bojan and back at Jovana. "Okay."

Jovana let her future sister-in-law help her from the floor. At that moment she made a promise to herself that she would never drink another drop until she died and went to be with the Lord.

She closed her eyes and prayed silently, "God, help me keep this vow."

*****

Kurt cursed the moment he woke the next morning. She'd never called him back. He needed to find out why. He would get dressed and go to *The Diner*, then he'd gently ask her why she hadn't called him last night. Maybe she hadn't gotten the message, but he doubted it because all night he'd sensed she wanted to be with him. That was why he'd asked her to call.

Last night, after imagining them together in bed and growing more frustrated by the minute, he turned on his computer for a little self-gratification. He figured it was better than letting the ache build until he went to a bar and did something stupid in anger. He eventually shut the computer down and went to sleep. Something had gone wrong with his plans and he intended to find out what it was.

After a cool shower, Kurt grabbed his most comfortable jeans and a tee shirt that fit him in a way that showed off the muscles he'd worked so hard to build. He glanced in the mirror and smiled at his reflection. He still had what it took to win a woman's heart. He just needed to use his assets more often.

Grabbing his jacket, he slipped it on. He scrubbed old Fred's head a few times, and walked out. He could hear his cat's loud mewing through the door of his apartment. Drat, he'd forgotten to feed the old boy. Ah well, that would come later. His fat cat was far from starving to death. Right now he had a certain delicate brunette to see and until they talked about why she hadn't called him last night, he wasn't coming back. He'd charm her until she agreed to go out with him today after work.

Yeah, soon she'd get her needs met even if she resisted him at first. He'd make sure she discovered that he could love her like no other man would. Then he'd fulfill his destiny with her. A shiver of delight shot through him as he climbed into his truck.

His pulse started racing at the thought of touching her, of being with her.

He'd win this time. Oh yeah, he'd win.

Let the games begin.

*****

Randy woke with a splitting headache. His stomach cramped like someone had reached inside his gut and started wringing his innards. Sweat rolled down his scalp into his eyes. He touched his forehead with the back of his hand. He was burning with a fever. He reached for his cell phone and called the restaurant to leave a message. No doubt Shep would be the first one to get it. Thankfully he'd thought ahead and let him keep the extra key.

"Yo!"

"Shep? It's Randy. What are you doing there already? We don't open for another hour."

"I know, boss, but I had a feeling I needed to come in early today. Call it institution."

"You mean intuition?" Randy closed his eyes. They burned like they were melting.

"Yeah, so what's up?" He heard Shep clear his throat and spit. Gross.

"I won't be in today. I've got a fever. Can you lock up and give Jovana a ride home after work? Her usual ride can't bring her home today so I told them I'd do it. But I'm too sick."

"No problemo, boss. It'd be my pleasure."

"Thanks." Randy hung up and closed his eyes, forcefully ignoring the strange tickling in his chest. Shep was up to something, but what? Hopefully he didn't have a thing for Jovana, too.

His muscles ached but he tried to sit up. Having no luck after several attempts, he flopped back down. He was too weak to get up from his bed to search for medicine that might help him fight this evil thing. He cursed the illness that attacked his body and interfered with his plans for the day.

As he drifted off, he thought about Jovana and how good she'd looked last night in that slinky black dress. How he wished he could see her today just to reassure her that she was okay with him. Maybe she'd already forgotten what she'd tried to do. But that conversation would have to come later, when he was well enough to think things through.

Right now he just felt like he was about to die, and ironically, if death approached him today he'd embrace it. He knew where he was going after he took his last breath.

But there was one thing he'd regret if he died today.

Leaving Jovana behind.

Chapter Seven

Jovana worked as hard as she could manage that morning so no one would believe she suffered from a hangover. She could still feel the lingering effects of too much wine, but for the most part she'd returned to normal. She had hoped to see Randy today to apologize if she'd acted inappropriately with him, but Shep had said he was at home with the flu. Hopefully they hadn't kissed, because most likely she would get it, too. If only she could remember what happened.

The front door chime dinged, indicating a new customer had arrived. Kurt strode in exuding sensual confidence. Oh my, but he was handsome. Genuinely glad to see him, she flashed him a bright smile to make up for not calling back.

He nodded, acknowledging her. But his face showed no humor.

"Hello! I get message but wallet is lost to me. I write number and put inside for keeping safe but is missing now. So sorry!"

"That's okay. The important thing is that I'm here now. So when do you get off your shift?"

She was getting better at understanding English every day, but she didn't know what he meant by shift and getting off of it, so she stared and waited for an explanation. None came. She sensed his growing irritation. "I not understand what means shift."

"Oh," he chuckled and stuffed his hands into his back pockets. "I meant when you are done working today. What time are you finished?"

Glancing at the clock, she answered him with a smile. "In thirty minutes. Is okay?"

"It's more than okay. I want to show you the thing I was talking about in my message."

"You mean surprise you haves for me? The one you say I like?"

"You remembered? That's great, honey."

"Yes. I remember." Her heart thumped with anticipation at the idea of being given a gift by someone she barely knew. A very handsome someone. But what would he give her? If that tender expression in his eyes meant anything, she figured it would be a kind gift. But what if she didn't want it? She'd just do what her mother always said to do, and that was to smile and say thank you regardless.

He slid onto a stool and grabbed a menu, then put it down without looking at it. His smile made her heart thump. He seemed to peer right into her soul as if trying to read her thoughts, and she liked it.

"I think you know what I want."

She saw the glimmer of mischief in his eyes and it made her think his words held a double meaning. Not that she minded. His attention flattered her, but she played dumb so he wouldn't know. "You want special breakfast? I am sorry but is too late in morning for ordering this."

He blinked, then quirked a grin. "You remembered what I like? Nice."

"Yes, I remember. Is coffee and muffin good for you?"

Glancing at her lips for just a moment, he met her eyes and muttered huskily, "Coffee is good, and I'd love to eat your muffin, hot stuff."

She smiled as she scribbled the muffin order on her pad and tore it off. He wanted his muffin heated up, which made sense. At least that's what she hoped he meant by hot stuff. She attached it to the order carousel in front of the cook's area and returned with a pot of decaf coffee.

"Regular, please."

She backed up and returned with the other pot. His intense look was making her nervous. Though she liked it, she could almost feel his eyes roaming over her.

He reached out and touched her hand that rested on the counter as she poured his coffee with the other. His thumb gently stroked her knuckles.

She glanced down. His gentle touch made her hand tingle, but the hair on the back of her neck rose at the same time. The bell on the front door of *The Diner* jingled and a cool gust of air blew inside as a customer left. It had to be a draft that pebbled her skin. She moved her hand out from under his and bit her lip, not sure if she should tell him to keep his hands to himself or encourage him to do it again. His attention both delighted and confused her.

The last customer left less than ten minutes later. Only twenty minutes until closing time.

She went into the kitchen to let the cook know they had no more customers, but he'd already clocked out. Shep often filled in after the cook left, so that didn't surprise her. He stood in the back room talking on his cell phone and he paced the floor like he was arguing with someone. He said something about money and not wanting to cheat someone. She didn't want to anger him by interrupting his conversation, so she started cleaning tables.

Kurt watched her for a few minutes while devouring his muffin. He licked his lips every time she looked in his direction. When he finished he smiled and brushed the moist crumbs from his fingers. He rubbed his palms together and said, "Mmmm... That was a really good muffin, babe."

The sincere compliment warmed her insides. She hadn't even made the muffins, or the coffee. He sure did know how to heat a woman's heart with a smile and a compliment. Georg had been charming when she'd first met him, too. But back then she'd been a naive teenager. She was older and wiser now. She would not let a man hurt her like Georg had done. Never again.

Once the other waitress clocked out, she noticed how he watched the clock and thrummed his fingers on the counter as if growing impatient. The minute it became closing time he turned the sign on the door so it read closed.

He started helping her straighten the napkins, refill the salt and pepper shakers, and roll the silverware without being asked. As they worked side by side, they snuck quick glances at each other. It was so nice of him to help her get things done so she could leave.

She was sure he was nothing like Georg.

After the last setting was done, she walked to the back to tell Shep she was ready to leave. She hadn't seen Laney yet but figured she was just running late.

He stopped talking and rested his palm over the phone. "Randy wanted me to tell you that your normal ride won't be bringing you home. He wanted me to give you a ride because he's sick today. If you don't mind waiting, I'm almost done with this call."

She glanced over her shoulder and quickly approached Kurt, who smiled at her.

"I can give you a ride home, honey."

It didn't take her long to decide to get a ride from Kurt. She wanted to see that surprise Kurt had mentioned and this would be the perfect way to spend time with him without her brother knowing about it. Shep looked too distracted to even notice who she left with. Perfect.

"Okay. I tell him I have ride home. Be back soon."

She tapped Shep on the shoulder. He'd started arguing again and she knew it might take awhile. She really wanted to go home before Laney got there. "I have ride with friend. Is okay. You not worry for me, yes?"

Shep nodded without looking at her, obviously too distracted by his conversation to care. It sounded like he spoke to a woman, but she didn't listen too closely because it wasn't her business.

Jovana removed her apron and hung it on a hook. She retrieved her street clothing from her locker and took the items to the bathroom to change.

*****

Kurt waited for her to emerge from the back room and shifted his feet when he thought about her changing her clothes. He wondered if she had any piercings or tattoos on that flawless skin. He'd always found tattoos sexy, but his former wife would never get one even though he'd practically begged her to. Another reason why he was glad she was gone from his life. She was too stubborn.

But he'd made her pay, just like he'd make Jovana pay if she defied him.

But enough of that negative thinking. Today was going to be an amazing day if he had anything to say about it. Nothing would spoil his good mood. Nothing.

His pants tightened in the front when he thought about his tattoo. He hoped to show it to Jovana later today. He'd had it drawn on a semi-private area below his hip and hovering just above his thigh. He only allowed certain women to see his nymph. Excitement and tension filled every muscle when he thought about how he'd have to be naked for her to see it. He shoved his hands in his front pockets and rocked on the balls of his feet. She was taking an awfully long time to get dressed.

He closed his eyes and thought about how she was going to be with him today.

Alone.

In his car.

How perfect was that?

A delightful shiver washed over him until he remembered his vow to take things slowly with her. Oh, he would try to get something from her today. He was just a man, not a saint. But if she wasn't ready yet he could wait for her a while longer. He just hoped it wouldn't take more than a few dates.

The moment she stepped into the main area of *The Diner* looking pretty enough to maul on the spot, he ripped his hands from his pockets. He longed to touch her, but forced himself to remain calm. As he scoured her from head to toe he smiled with appreciation. That tight pink tee shirt with candy hearts on it and those low hip-hugging jeans were a yummy combination. Maybe she was trying to tell him something. Would she give him a taste of her sweetness today?

She pulled her jacket on, revealing her tiny navel. No piercing or tattoo that he could see. Regardless, her toned stomach looked so delicious he struggled to contain his response.

Shoving his hands into his front pockets, he hoped she hadn't caught how just seeing her wearing her street clothes made him hard. If she noticed his body's response she might guess what he'd planned to try the moment they were alone.

He must've been ogling a bit too intensely because she seemed suddenly nervous and her cheeks flushed. Her eyes scanned his body and landed on his zipper.

She'd noticed the tightness. This excited him and worried him at the same time.

Calm down, Kurt. Don't blow your chances. She's the one and she's worth waiting for.

He offered her the most disarming smile he could muster. "My you clean up nice."

Her brow furrowed and she pursed her luscious lips as her gaze dragged from his zipper back to his eyes. A confused expression teased her face. "Yes, I have shower today."

A laugh burst from him when he realized how literally she took everything he said. Some of their communication must be lost in the translation. "You do smell good, honey."

"Thank you." She bit her lip. A simple gesture, but it looked incredibly sensual.

He stepped back and held the door for her, hoping for patience, but knowing it would be a fierce battle for him to wait. "After you, my darling."

She giggled. "You don't know me and you call honey and darling. Is funny customs."

Her teasing tone rubbed him the wrong way, but he chose to ignore his reaction and continue playing the game. He would get through to her heart if it killed him... or he'd silence her for good.

But not until he got what he wanted first. And boy, did he want her.

As she strolled in front of him he fought to keep his tongue in his mouth. While her face wasn't as pretty as his Mary's had been, her body rocked. That made up for some of the other areas that she lacked. The fact that she was so tiny only made the art of seduction easier for him. He could overpower her with one hand tied behind his back and blindfolded. The challenge would be to get it from her willingly. That would be more exciting than forcing her to comply.

He gazed at her perfect legs. Though her muscles appeared nice and toned under her clothing, she didn't give him the impression she could do much damage if she were to fight him. Hopefully that wouldn't be necessary. He didn't want to bruise that lovely olive skin.

She glanced around the parking lot and stopped. "Is that you truck?"

He nodded in the direction she pointed and strolled over to his vehicle so he could open her door. She waited for him like any properly trained woman would. Smiling, he made sure she was comfortable in her seat. He shivered from the curious look in her eyes as he locked her door.

As he climbed into his seat and clipped on his belt, he asked, "How much time do you have to spend with me?"

"Not too much. I think Laney bring me, but she haves Randy drive. But he is sick."

"Can I take you on a long drive before we head to your place?"

"If is not too long, then is okay. Maybe one hour? She be home soon and I must be home first."

"I think I can do that. We'll be there shortly."

He paused for a moment and decided to pray before he drove. If nothing else it would convince her that he was safe. "Can I pray for you before we leave?"

"Yes." She reached for his hands and smiled at him like he hung the moon. His heart grew warm and tingly inside. Terror yanked the breath from his lungs. He was falling for this woman in a way he hadn't expected. How could he hurt her if he had feelings for her?

The answer to his question came quickly, telling him he was still in control. If she behaved he wouldn't have to hurt her. It was her choice. Her fate. He didn't decide that, she did.

She bowed her head and closed her eyes.

"God, keep us safe as we travel down the road a little ways. Amen."

He squeezed her hand and she reciprocated. Then he risked rejection and kept his hand covering hers. She accepted him, shooting a thrill through his veins from his head to his feet.

As they held hands and drove toward the San Pedro River, she didn't question him further. She just looked out the window and smiled like she enjoyed the scenery. Everything was brown this time of year, so it wasn't that great to look at. Maybe she was smiling because she was happy to be with him.

Closing her eyes, she whispered, "Is peaceful."

Good, she felt comfortable enough to relax with him. And while he really wanted to stroke her knuckles, he held back. He didn't want to seem too forward. "I'm taking you to see your surprise, just in case you wondered why we're driving away from your road."

"This is what I think you do. I trust you. So how you know where my house is?"

"I saw you once when I was visiting a friend down the street from you. You were getting out of an SUV with a lady who looks a lot like you."

"Ah. That is my sister-in-law. Her wedding to brother is next week. She goes to Tucson for things buy for wedding so she is gone most days."

He let go of her hand and reached across her thighs. He pulled open the glove box. "Mind if I have a smoke?"

She wrinkled her nose. "Smokes make me sneeze. I do not like smoke."

Shutting the compartment, he sighed. "I won't smoke around you. I want you to be happy."

Cocking her head, she peered at him closely. She touched his arm, and asked, "Why you care for me what I think?"

"Isn't it obvious? You're a beautiful woman and I want to get to know you better."

"But why is this?" Her tiny nose wrinkled as she squinted at him.

He wasn't sure how to answer that so with mild irritation he replied with his own question. "Does it matter? Don't you want to know me better?"

She scanned his face for a moment and answered, "Yes."

His heart responded in a delicious, yet frightening way that felt an awful lot like love. He couldn't get attached to her. Not like this. It would ruin everything.

Absolutely everything.

*****

Randy tossed on his bed. Something disturbed his rest. Something more than the raging fever and chills. Something dark and sinister had stolen his peace. He opened his eyes and the word that slipped from his lips was, "Jovana."

Not sure why he couldn't break his mind free from her image, he took it as a sign that she needed prayer. Sensing she was in trouble, he began to pray like he'd never prayed before. After releasing an emphatic amen, he fell back on his bed, too weak to pick up the phone to check on her.

"Lord, please keep her safe."

Chapter Eight

Jovana glanced over at Kurt as he drove. She felt so *umoren,* so tired. So weak. Thankfully she didn't feel afraid. He'd done nothing to make her suspect he would harm her. In fact, he'd said he wanted to get to know her better. The feeling was mutual. And he smelled so manly, so good. At first the sight of his arousal had made her nervous, but then she realized it was a natural response to seeing an attractive woman. Men couldn't help it, so she wouldn't hold that against him.

After what seemed like forever, Kurt pulled up onto a dirt road and parked off to the side. It looked like a tiny, deserted town. "This is *iznenaduvanje?*"

He looked at her like she'd lost her mind. "What?"

"I am sorry. I should say in English. I ask this is surprise?"

Kurt stretched and placed his arm behind her. He covered her shoulder with his palm and gently squeezed. "Yep. I discovered it my first week in town and thought it was awesome so I wanted to share it with you. Do you like it?"

"What is this place?"

"It's a ghost town called Fairbanks."

"A ghost town? Is haunted?"

"No, that just means it's deserted."

"Is in desert, yes. So you live here?" Why would he take her to a ghost town in the desert? What a strange *podarok,* gift.

"No. I live near your brother." He pointed. "Look, there's a caretaker that maintains the buildings on site, but he lives way back there, so we're all alone. Would you like to see everything?"

"Okay. I like to see this." She wasn't sure what he was up to, but didn't have the strength to fight him right now. She waited until he opened her door and helped her out. Her muscles ached and her head felt like someone was poking it with an ice pick. The headache felt very different from the one she'd received from her hangover. This headache made her wince. But she didn't want to spoil things so she tried to act like she felt great.

"You winced. Did I hurt your hand?" He bent and looked down at her so they were at eye level. "I'm sorry. Sometimes I don't know my own strength."

"No, is headache from lights. Is no big deal. Rest fixes later."

"Okay, so it's like a migraine?"

She didn't know what that was so she just clutched her head and frowned. "I do not know."

"Don't worry. We won't stay long." He tugged her hand and walked her over to the old schoolhouse building like an eager child.

He was acting strangely. Too happy and energetic. Something wasn't right.

Her head began spinning. She dug in her heels and tugged on his arm. "Please. Stop."

The man halted and turned to face her. He got down on one knee and peered into her eyes. He held her face and his gentle touch soothed her. "Are you sure you're all right?"

"I do not know." Her eyes filled with tears and she suddenly felt like she just wanted to sleep.

Touching her neck with his hands, he muttered, "You feel a little hot."

A whimper escaped her as the pounding grew more intense. She closed her eyes and felt his lips on her forehead, then her cheek, and slowly moving down her neck. She shuddered and put her palm out to keep him from getting any closer. While it felt *simpatichno* nice, the timing wasn't right. She hurt too much to enjoy his kisses. "Please, no."

He tipped her chin up. She opened her eyes and he gazed at her like he wanted to *bakni*, to kiss her mouth this time. But her eyes burned and her stomach started to cramp. "I am sorry. I feel sick, like I haves *grip*, flu."

His hands slid down her back until his palms pressed against her bottom and he pulled her close, ignoring what she'd said. While his gentle touch felt good, the pain from her stomach made everything seem very distant. The earth started spinning.

She could feel his hands squeezing her bottom as his lips grazed her neck and he moaned. "You're so beautiful..."

A sour taste suddenly filled her mouth and she salivated. Without having a moment to plan her response, she shoved him away from her and vomited on the ground beside him. Some of her stomach contents splashed onto his shoes. She barely caught her breath and vomited again.

"What the--" He started cursing. She didn't speak English very well, but she knew bad swear words when she heard them.

"I'm sorry. So sorry." Clutching her stomach she fought another wave of nausea and the sob that crept up her throat. She hated vomiting more than anything. "I think I sick. Get from Randy. Please, take me home."

He grabbed her shoulders and gently shook her. "Were you screwing him? Is that how you got sick? Tell me!"

She cried softly, not understanding his sudden anger. She had no idea what he meant about screwing or why he was so angry with her. His sudden change in behavior reminded her of Georg. A cold chill zipped down her spine until she started trembling uncontrollably. "No. Please, no. I do not know what you speak of."

He paused as if he wasn't sure he believed her, but then touched her cheek like a concerned father. Something else Georg used to do. He'd lash out one minute and then coddle her the next. His behavior used to confuse her so much she thought she was going crazy. Like now.

"Let's get you home in bed, honey. We can come back here when you're feeling better, okay?"

All she could do was nod and thank God that he agreed to drive her home. She couldn't handle more because of the merciless hammering in her skull. Soon she'd be in bed and right now she couldn't think of a single place she'd rather be.

*****

Randy woke the next morning feeling a little bit better, but he was still too sick to go to work. What he had went beyond mere food poisoning. He was pretty sure he had the flu. Hopefully Jovana felt okay and hadn't caught anything from him.

Releasing an exhausted sigh, he reached for his cell phone and saw that the battery had nearly run out overnight. He needed to charge it, but it would take too much energy to get up and plug it in. He dialed *The Diner* hoping to find her there.

"Shep here."

"Thank God you're in. I'm still too sick to come to work."

"Sorry to hear that."

"Is Jovana at work today?"

"Haven't seen her. Bojan called and said she wouldn't be in. I guess she has the flu, too."

Randy sighed. "I was afraid that would happen."

Shep chuckled. "You think you gave it to her?"

"Probably." Randy closed his eyes and prayed she'd recover quickly.

"You didn't do the nasty with her, did you, boss?"

"The what? No. I haven't touched her that way. I can't believe you'd even say that."

"But you know you want to." Shep's chuckling sounded more like coughing. He was probably smoking inside the kitchen even though it was against the law.

"And I'll bet that guy who keeps coming around to see her would love to get some action, too. I would try myself, but the Mrs. would throw me out."

"What guy? What does he look like?"

Shep chuckled. "Tall, mid-thirties, clean-shaven. Leather jacket."

Randy groaned. That same guy was still coming around. "Has he come by lately?"

"So far I haven't seen him today. But he offered to drive her home yesterday."

66

Panic constricted Randy's throat. "Tell me you didn't let him."

"I was busy and she didn't want to wait. She seemed happy about going with him."

"Of course she did. She probably thought she could trust him."

"I didn't see any reason to worry. She's been talking to him for over a week now. He seems like just a regular guy. She's a grown woman who can make her own choices."

"I know, but I have a bad feeling about him." Randy sighed. "Thanks for telling me. Next time you take her home. You got that?"

"You want me, the ex-con, to take your boss's sister home? Are you sure Bojan would even be okay with that? You know how he feels about me."

"Bojan worries about everything. I'm not worried about you. It's that stranger who scares me."

"Maybe you should be worried," Shep muttered.

"Huh?" Did you say something?" Randy yawned. He couldn't believe how exhausted he felt.

"Nothing. See you when you're feeling better."

"Bye." Randy turned the phone off and set it on the table by his bed. Sleep quickly overtook him until a frightening thought burned through his muscles. And like a cannonball, he shot from his bed. Sick or not, he needed to make sure Jovana was okay.

And what about Laney? If she got sick it would ruin their wedding plans.

Randy dialed Laney's number and waited.

"Hello?"

"Laney? Are you okay? I heard Jovana has the flu now, too."

"Yes, she does, the poor thing. I've been wearing a mask over my face and scrubbing down the walls and surfaces to try and protect myself from getting the flu virus before our wedding. Bojan is frantic that his sister is sick and he's just as worried that I'll contract whatever she has."

"I can help you out. I'm already sick so I can't get it any worse."

"Oh, would you, Randy? That's so great of you to offer! I'll call Bojan right now and let him know that you'll stay with Jovana a few days until you have both recovered. I'll take my things to a weekly rental in town. Bojan is going to be so happy to hear this! Thank you so much!"

"No problem."

Laney hung up

Randy lay there and processed what had just taken place. Had he just offered to play Jovana's nursemaid for the rest of the week? Was he crazy? While he was glad to help out, he worried that she might take it the wrong way, especially given the way she'd acted the other night. But she probably didn't even remember what happened.

He wanted to help her and if it also helped his boss then he didn't see any reason to be worried. He would do whatever was necessary to make her feel safe and protected while she recovered. It was the least he could do to show her that he was nothing like that sick-o Georg that she kept referring to. He would show her how a man is supposed to treat a woman.

She would never fear him.

*****

Randy rang the doorbell to Laney's home and shivered. He was still feverish and wondered why he had agreed to such a crazy plan. He should be home in bed right now drinking fluids and taking medication for his own aches and pains, not standing outside waiting to take care of a sick woman.

Laney answered the door. She wore a surgical mask just like she'd told him. She also wore gloves like dentists used when they cleaned a patient's teeth. Sheesh, you'd think he and Jovana had the plague or something.

"I'm so glad you're here. Bojan is thrilled you're willing to help out, too."

"I'm glad to." He lifted the plastic grocery bag he carried and showed it to Laney. "I even brought my own pharmacy, and I'm willing to share."

"That's good. She's been whimpering for the past few hours and I don't know how to help her. I've given her fever reducer and cooled her off the best I could. I've set clear soda by her bed and crackers in case she gets hungry. I've prayed for the past thirty minutes."

"Sounds like you've done a great job so far. I think I can take it from here. Just show me where I'm supposed to be staying and I'll get settled in."

Laney walked him up the stairs and pointed at a door. "You'll stay in this guest bedroom. Jovana's room is right across the hall. That way if she needs something you'll hear her."

"Isn't that kind of close?" He peeked into the room and saw her sleeping soundly.

"It's the only guest room on this floor and I slept in it last night. I'm sorry, but she was up once or twice an hour and you can't help her if you sleep all the way downstairs. I made the bed up with fresh sheets and everything."

"It just feels kind of weird to be sleeping so near her. I'll get over it. Don't mind me."

Laney touched his bicep with her rubber gloved hand. "I really appreciate this. I know it's kind of awkward with you being her boss and everything, but we don't know anyone else who knows Macedonian as well as you do who can help take care of her."

"I understand. I'm by no means fluent, but I get by fine."

"Exactly. And she's been muttering in her own language for an hour now. I have no clue what she is saying and Bojan just went into a meeting a few hours ago so I can't call him to interpret."

"I'll do what I can. I'm not one hundred percent myself, but I was coherent enough to drive here so I'm functional at least. I just need a few more days of rest and I'll be back to my usual ornery self."

"I've prayed for her and explained to her that someone was going to come and stay with her for a few days and take good care of her. She was so out of it I doubt she understood a word. Thanks again, Randy. You're the best!"

"You're delusional if you think there is anything good in me."

Laney smiled. "You are a kind hearted man, Randy Strong. Don't worry, I know it's Christ in you." Chuckling, she headed into her bedroom and emerged with a suitcase and her purse.

Randy peered into the guest room where he'd be sleeping. It looked cozy and inviting. He turned back to say something to her when a worried frown appeared on Laney's face.

"Are you concerned about leaving her now that you're free to go?"

Laney's face relaxed a bit. "How'd you know?"

"I can read you like a book. Now go and keep yourself healthy for your wedding, young lady."

"Thanks again. I can never repay you for this." Laney's eyes glistened.

"Your thanks is enough. Now don't get me started with those tears. I'm a sensitive guy."

With a reluctant nod, Laney whispered a prayer for them both and slipped into the hallway.

He chuckled and unpacked the few things he'd brought and set them on the dresser. After he situated his belongings, he peeked in on Jovana one more time and saw that she was still asleep. For that moment she looked peaceful. The covers came up to her chin, and though she was a bit sweaty, she didn't look flushed and feverish. The medication must've kicked in.

Stretching to work out the knots in his muscles, he stepped into the hall and headed for the guest room. On the way he erupted into a lengthy yawn and decided to climb in bed and get a bit of rest while he still could. Pulling down the covers, he slipped between the sheets. The soft material against his skin made him sigh deeply with contentment. As he inhaled he pulled in the scent of freshly laundered sheets. Too bad he was so sick; otherwise the experience would be even more heavenly.

Closing his eyes, he imagined lying next to Jovana and holding her close. His neck heated when he thought about how Jovana only slept in the other room. He thought about climbing into her bed and loving on her. But she was sick, so he forced the tempting thoughts from his mind.

Besides the fact that it would be wrong, she'd probably hate him for even thinking such a thing.

But that didn't stop him from wanting to be with her. He rolled over and punched his pillow. Seconds later, he flipped onto his back. Releasing a groan, he rubbed his eyes and prayed for rest.

Something told him it was going to be a very long night.

Chapter Nine

Randy woke after what seemed like only minutes of rest. He tossed in bed and finally threw the sheets off when he got them untangled. The sound of coyotes howling outside the window combined with his aching muscles made it difficult to sleep. He had never realized how much quieter it was in the foothills at night compared to living in the city. Tonight the wild creatures sparring outside drowned out the silence.

He got up to use the bathroom. His mouth was so dry that his lips stuck to his teeth. Turning on the tap water, he filled a cup and drank the icy water as he waited for the heater to warm it up. Then he gargled and spit into the sink. The moment the water reached a pleasant temperature he washed his face.

Deciding to check on Jovana, he splashed water on his cheeks and rinsed off the soap. He prayed she would soon be on the mend. It had grieved his heart to see her so tiny and vulnerable on that twin mattress when Laney had showed him the bedrooms. He wanted to see Jovana again. To make sure she was comfortable despite the sickness that ravaged them both.

He dried his face and stepped into the hallway. Some strange sounds now blended with the cackling coyotes. They resembled frenzied whimpers, like a wounded animal fighting to spring from a trap that had crushed its paw. Stepping lightly over to the bedroom Jovana slept in, he cracked the door and peeked inside.

She tossed in the bed, obviously feverish again. Muttering words in Macedonian, she struggled and pulled at the sheets as she cried. He listened closely and tried to translate what she said.

"No. Please don't make me do this. I beg you. Please. I will do anything if you don't make me do this. Of course, I love you. I would not be here if I did not love you. If you love me, you will not make me do this. No, I did not mean it that way... Of course, you are right. Yes, you are always right... I am just stupid. I did not mean to disobey you. I was afraid... Please, no. I'm sorry. Have mercy on me. I will listen better next time. Please. Oh God, forgive me..."

Her words slurred and jumbled together, wrapping around her sobs until they became almost indiscernible. He listened closely as the pitch of her voice grew louder and he debated on whether or not he should wake her up to free her from the upsetting dream.

"Please do not leave me. I said I was wrong. I will do whatever you say, I promise. I will starve if you do not help me. Please. For the sake of your child do not do this to me. Of course this is your child. I would not lie to you. I cannot... no... this is not right... please... help me... I am not ready to die... Please, someone help me. God, do not let me die this way."

A lump filled his throat as he approached her with caution. He didn't want her to confuse him with whoever plagued her dreams -- probably the Georg guy she'd told him about. He'd never met the man, but hated him for the emotional damage he'd done to Jovana.

He sat in the chair and reached for a cloth in case her fever had risen. He dipped it into the bowl of water that sat on the dresser next to the bed. He marveled at what she'd said. She had a child? Where? Sweat had beaded on her forehead and above her lip as she tossed back and forth on her pillow. Reaching first for her arm, he touched her gently and whispered in Macedonian, "You're safe now, dear friend. I will take care of you. You have nothing to fear anymore."

Jovana's features softened instantly and her whimpers ceased. "Thank you."

He touched her forehead with the cool cloth and she gasped slightly, but resumed resting. The soft breaths she took made him smile. Even in her sleep she appeared delicate. Whatever plagued her dreams didn't seem to be related to the fever. Maybe she had memories that crept into her mind while she slept. He had the same thing happen to him. Every now and then he'd dream about the night those thugs cracked his skull at the restaurant. The night the waitress had been sexually assaulted and he could hear her cries through the haze of his head injury. But in his dreams he'd always saved her from those demons. If only dreams came true.

He'd fix things for Jovana somehow. He would not let anyone hurt the little bird nestled in the bed beside his chair. She would not be harmed as long as he was able to protect her. Even if she didn't want him to keep an eye on her, he would still do that to make sure she was safe. He didn't want to risk another woman he cared about getting hurt. And the way Bojan acted with his sister told Randy that his boss must also know something about her past that made him overprotective.

She sighed as he gently massaged her forehead with the damp cloth. He hated to wake her to take more medication to reduce her fever. Right now it wasn't too bad. As he debated what to do next she shifted and the light blanket covering her pajamas fell away. He could see through the wet clothing. The outline of her breasts made his neck heat.

The damp material clung to her and no doubt would chill her eventually if she kept the damp nightgown touching her skin. A shiver emitted from her as if to confirm his worries. Her skin pebbled under her clothing and she writhed as she struggled to pull the blanket over herself again. The moment she managed to cover herself she relaxed. She had yet to open her eyes.

He stroked her cheek and rested his palm against her smooth skin for a moment. She placed her hand over his, her eyes still closed as she sighed. He paused and waited to see what she would say.

"I'm thirsty..." Her Macedonian accent made warm tingles travel from head to toe. Or he could be getting his fever back. That had to be it.

He muttered comforting words and reached for the water beside her bed. He didn't know how to say sip in Macedonian so he just said *ispie*, which means drink up, or drink.

A slight nod of her head told him that she'd heard him. However, she still didn't move or open her eyes. He slid his hand under her neck and slowly raised her to a sitting position.

"*Fala*, thanks," she whispered.

He tipped the glass just enough for her to get a sip of water. After she drank it she just rested her head on his hand, her eyes still closed. He set the cup down and brushed her cheek with the tips of his fingers. Her damp hair now clung to her forehead, so he nudged it away before pressing a light kiss on her cheek. Then he planted another kiss on her opposite cheek.

She smiled, her eyes still shut, and said in Macedonian, "Thank you for your kindness."

He found the softness etched on her face difficult to resist. Before he could talk himself out of it, he gently kissed her forehead, but lingered this time. He returned her from the upright position to lying flat on her back. Her eyes remained closed, but a peaceful smile appeared on her face. At the same time a tiny tear spilled down her cheek. He brushed it away with his thumb and prayed that the Lord would give her peace. She reached for his hand and rested it over her heart, her eyes still closed.

Did she even know it was him? Or did she think someone else had come to her aid? He doubted that Laney had told Jovana he was coming over. So who did she believe was with her and now tended her needs? His eyes moistened as he thought about what she'd just done to demonstrate her complete trust in him. It surprised him to feel tears welling in his eyes because he'd never gotten emotional over a woman before. Not for any reason.

While guilt consumed him over the assault on his waitress and he'd cried after he found out she was raped, that was very different. What he felt for Jovana was more like deep affection. It made his heart weep tears of sorrow mixed with an intense longing to make her life different. Better.

So why did he care so much about this delicate flower? Was it because she seemed to need protecting? Surely that wouldn't be the only reason he felt so drawn to her.

She shivered again and muttered in her native tongue, "I need to get this wet clothing off. Can you please help me, Georg?"

Everything warm inside of him went cold. She thought he was that beast Georg.

Her hands moved to the front of her pajamas and she started unbuttoning her nightgown. Panic rose in his throat. Now what was he supposed to do? She needed to get out of her wet clothes but he didn't want to see her without them on. Well, actually he did want to see her that way. He just knew that it wouldn't be right in God's eyes. He needed to protect his mind, so as much as it killed him to resist, staring at her body would have to be off limits.

It suddenly struck him that he could cover her with a dry sheet and move her over to his bed. So he darted over to the linen closet and grabbed a clean, dry sheet. Her eyes still closed, she started working her shoulders out of the gown. Her pretty little moan sounded so sensual he had to force himself to focus on her needs rather than his desire. He gently draped the sheet over her. Once it became apparent that she had slipped out of the soaked gown, he scooped her up in the dry sheet and moved her to his guest bed. She weighed no more than a sack of potatoes and she looked so pale, so weak. Still delirious, she obviously had no idea he was even there.

Slipping her under the covers wearing only the sheet he'd draped over her, he prayed that she would not make a wrong assumption when she finally came to and found herself naked in his bed. What a disaster that would be if his boss found out. He went back into her bedroom and stripped the soaked sheets and nightgown from the bed. He then started a load of laundry. As he turned the knob to start the washer, he realized that his fever had fully returned, so he went back upstairs and grabbed some medicine. He prayed for healing and downed the drugs with a glass of water.

Exhaustion overtook him again and he decided to lie down and rest. But first he needed to remake her bed. Maybe he could slip her back into it and she'd never know the difference. He finished making the twin bed and pulled the sheets down. When he entered his guest room to retrieve Jovana he found her rolled on to her side and he could see her bare back. A cluster of faded lines covered her upper shoulders. When he peered closer he saw that they were scars, like someone had beaten her with a stick. Her hair normally covered that part of her back, which explained why he hadn't seen the marks before. He wondered if Bojan knew about them. That might explain why he seemed so paranoid about her relationships with men. Did he know that Georg had mistreated her?

She rolled onto her back and he saw her exposed breasts. She was even more beautiful than he'd imagined. Heat shot through him and he exhaled loudly, "God help me."

Before he could look away, her eyes popped open. She must've heard him. When she found him staring at her she screamed and covered her body with the sheet. "Why you in bedroom? Get out!"

"I was just--"

"Get out!"

He clamped his lips shut and left the room in a hurry before she threw something at him. What a lousy time for her to wake up. He hadn't planned to see her naked and had taken every precaution to avoid that. Regardless, he'd still seen more of her than he'd intended. He couldn't believe that even though the entire situation had only lasted a few awkward seconds, she'd actually caught him staring. Lord only knew what she thought about him right now. Probably that he'd undressed her and taken advantage of her.

With a groan, he retreated to the bedroom she had been sleeping in and glanced at the bed that he'd made up fresh. He started to shut the door so he could lie down, but the door flung open and hit the wall with a thud.

Jovana stood in nothing but a sheet wrapped around her thin frame, and with wide, wet eyes she held the sheet in front of her and pointed at the door. "You go to you bed and I go for my bed. Now!"

Randy didn't hesitate or try to argue with her. He was smarter than that, so he left the room immediately, not wanting to get in any more trouble that he was already in. He still couldn't believe how things had turned around so quickly. Now she probably hated him and thought the worst of him.

He groaned. How was he going to fix this problem without divine intervention? Truth was he didn't think it was possible. So rather than torture himself with guilt even though he'd done nothing wrong, Randy laid down on the bed Jovana had vacated and closed his burning eyes. He prayed his fever would respond to the medicine and ease up because he was tired of being sick.

Preferring to imagine himself well again, he thought about spending time with Jovana in the near future as she talked about her life. He wanted to ask about her child. A satisfied smile tugged his mouth and he imagined kissing her and holding her close. Lord willing, he'd find a way to help her see that she could trust him or that would never happen. Not as long as she thought he was a jerk like her ex.

Within minutes, he fell fast asleep.

*****

Kurt glanced at the clock and groaned. Time to go to work.

But how was he supposed to lift things when he felt like crud? He could barely raise his head from the pillow. He rose from his bed, determined to give it a try, but his stomach started churning as he strolled into the living room.

Better call in. He pushed his cat from his chair and reached for the phone. It slipped from his fingers and hit the floor. With a groan he reached for it and finally dialed his work number.

"Marvin's Movers... We'll move anything for the right price. How can I help you today?"

"Marge? It's Kurt. I feel like I'm gonna hurl and my body aches everywhere. I think I caught the flu from my girlfriend."

"You and half the crew. This flu season is the worst ever."

His muscles tensed. Jovana hadn't given half the crew the flu. He knew it was just a lame expression. But if he ever found out she was sleeping around that would be the end of her life as she knew it. He'd make sure she knew why she was being punished, too. But enough paranoia. As far as he could tell she wasn't interested in anyone else.

"You get some rest. Ya hear?"

"Yeah." He coughed. "If you don't see me in a few days send for an ambulance."

"You got it. Thanks for not coming in and giving your germs to the few of us who are still healthy in this place."

"No problem. See you hopefully tomorrow."

"You get better. If you need anything just call Marge here. I'll take care of you."

"Thanks. Will do." He groaned and fell back in the chair, too weak to get up and go back to bed. Maybe he'd rest right here for a few minutes. He couldn't remember ever feeling this sick before. He wanted to call Jovana and thank her for blessing him with the plague, but only after cussing her out. Then again, he was the one who'd insisted on kissing her. If he'd kept a distance from her he wouldn't feel like death warmed over right now. He only had himself to blame.

He couldn't tell half the time if he was freezing or sweating. He'd thoroughly soaked the clothes he'd worn to bed, so he pulled off the wet tee shirt sticking to his chest. A shiver zipped through him and he forced himself up from the chair. As he stumbled toward the bedroom he grabbed a quilt from the closet. His apartment wasn't much to look at, but it was practical. Right now he needed the walls to lean on, so he wasn't complaining.

Thankfully his health insurance benefits had kicked in now that he'd been in his position for the required thirty days. Hopefully he wouldn't need to use it, but if the magnitude of his headache and the soreness in his muscles was any indication, he'd be calling a doctor soon. Too bad he hadn't thought to find a primary care doctor before he actually needed one. They probably couldn't help him anyway.

He wished he had some fever medicine, but since he didn't have any on hand he'd have to sweat it out. With a grunt, he hauled the blanket up as he climbed into bed. He arranged it so it covered him and hoped it would reduce his shivering. Curling up in a fetal position seemed to help, so he tucked his chin to his knees and closed his burning eyes.

Images of Jovana's face and lithe body danced across his vision. He determined to have sweet dreams as he thought about seeing her and kissing her from head to toe. Something told him if he did this her response would be so enthusiastic it would blow his mind. He wanted to see her so badly he could feel the anticipation building up and transmitting to his body despite chills from the flu.

If he felt well enough tomorrow he'd send her flowers and wish her a speedy recovery. That would help regain her trust. He needed to get back on track with his plans.

Women adored flowers, right? Yeah, that's what he'd do.

*****

Jovana sat up and immediately noticed a vase of yellow roses on her dresser. She couldn't recall seeing them before, but then again she'd been so sick that the past several days were a total blur. She did remember Laney leaving and Randy coming to stay with her, but the details were very fuzzy.

Her fever had finally ended when the muscle aches and vomiting had ceased the previous evening. So far today the sun hadn't risen, but she decided to crawl out of bed anyway.

First, she wanted to read the card that came with the roses. Laney had probably sent them, but part of her hoped Kurt had something to do with the flowers. Pulling the card from the tiny envelope she saw neat printing. She didn't recognize the writing as Laney's or her brother's.

She translated the English words. *Get well soon, honey. Your new friend, Kurt.*

Smiling because she could actually read his kind words, she replaced the card and inhaled the fragrant scent exuding from the roses. How nice of him to send her flowers. If they were intended to cheer her today they'd done the trick.

So sick of feeling sick, she wanted to call Laney and let her know she was healthy enough to attend the wedding in a few days. She also wanted to thank Kurt for the flowers, but realized she still didn't have his number. Not unless Randy had brought her wallet inside with him.

But first she needed a shower and to freshen up before she talked to Kurt, Randy, or anyone else. If she couldn't stand her own smell, no doubt it would offend others.

She vaguely remembered Randy being in the house and Laney whispering to her that he'd be there for a few days. She understood why Laney wouldn't want to risk getting the *grip*, the flu right before her wedding, so she didn't take offense.

While the urge to peek and see if he was in the other room was strong, she decided against it. Now greasy, her hair needed a good washing. She had so many knots and tangles she worried she would have to get her hair cut in order to comb through her locks with ease.

As the hot water washed over her she released a contented sigh. It felt good to wash the sticky sweat from her skin. She shampooed twice and let the conditioner soak in before she rinsed it out. A hint of coconut wafted in the air and she savored the scent along with her renewed health.

It wasn't until the water turned cold that she realized she had stayed in the shower way too long. Releasing a tiny yelp, she turned the knob and shut off the water. She glanced at her hand, which had wrinkled too. As she dried off she listened closely and realized that the dogs were barking but they sounded far off, like they were outside. Panic zipped through her chest and she quickly patted the moisture from her skin.

What if the *kuches*, dogs had gotten out while she was asleep? If anything happened to Laney's Chihuahuas she'd be in so much trouble. She pulled on a sweat suit and frowned when she saw how loose it had gotten because of her illness. She needed to check on the dogs and find something to eat that would restore her strength.

Through the tiny slats in the window blinds she caught a glimpse of the sun's rays streaking through the windows. She couldn't help wondering if Randy was still there or if he'd gone to work and left her in the house alone. She grabbed a wide toothed comb and worked on the snarls in her hair as she walked down the hallway to the guest bedroom.

Pausing in the hallway when she saw that the door was open a crack, she gently pushed to open it further. The image of Randy lying in bed sound asleep imprinted in her mind. He looked so kind even in his sleep. So why had she found him ogling her when she was *gol*, naked, a few days ago? Did he have a sinister side that she was about to discover, or was there a rational reason for it? Maybe she had imagined the whole thing, but she doubted it. Something told her it was real.

"Ron-dee?" she whispered, hoping to wake him without startling him.

His eyes fluttered open and he looked around as if trying to orient himself to his surroundings. When his gaze landed on Jovana's eyes, he smiled. "You're looking much better."

She approached him and raked the wet comb through her hair, purposely shedding some droplets of water on Randy in the process.

He sucked in a breath and hollered, "Man, that's cold!"

A giggle escaped her and she stepped back. "Sorry!"

"You are *so* not sorry and you know it."

Biting the inside of her cheek, she kept silent as she admired his face. He looked sexy in a rugged way with that fresh growth of whiskers.

She'd never seen him with facial hair before, let alone the beginnings of a beard. It looked nice.

He sat up and watched her in silence as she combed through the rest of her hair. He held the comforter up to his neck so it covered him. She no longer heard the dogs yipping and remembered her plan to check on them. "I need for check dogs."

"They're fine. I put them in the game room last night so they wouldn't wreck the house and they'd be warm. So who gave you the roses?"

She blinked. "Kurt gives me flowers."

"Kurt? Who is that?"

"He is friend. You do not know him." Technically that was true. He knew of Kurt, but didn't know him personally. Hopefully he wouldn't ask her to expound on this.

"I don't?"

"No." She wasn't sure what to say next, so she waited.

"Would you like some breakfast?" Randy rubbed his eyes.

"Yes! I love *jajtse*."

"I think there are eggs in the fridge. Want me to make you some?"

"Yes, please." She smiled and clutched her hands behind her back so she wouldn't reach out and touch him. "I like beard. Is very handsome."

He peered at her from the corner of his eye. "Thanks."

She bit her lip to keep from saying more. Why did she have to tell her boss she thought he was handsome? She didn't want to give him any ideas.

Randy slid over and placed his feet on the floor, the comforter still covering him. He peered at her and she turned to look at the wall. But she could still see him from the corner of her eye. In one quick move he whisked his sweatpants from the floor and pulled them on. His bare chest was now exposed and she couldn't help appreciating his build. Georg hadn't looked nearly as good when he was half dressed. Not even when she'd still loved him. She couldn't help smiling at her thoughts, bizarre as it was to compare the two men. They were nothing alike.

Sometimes Kurt reminded her of Georg, but mostly in a good way. So far Kurt seemed more good than not. When she was sick she vaguely remembered him bringing her home and kissing her gently. She also remembered throwing up on his shoes and how that upset him. Would Randy get upset if she did the same thing? Surely he'd know she couldn't help it and would be more understanding.

Since when had she started liking Randy? She nearly laughed aloud at the thought. Then she remembered the night he brought her home and her stomach flipped. "I must apologize for night I drink wine. I hope I not offensive for you."

"You didn't offend me." His warm smile told her he meant what he said.

He stood and his bare chest was now inches from her lips. She inhaled his manly scent and tried to focus on his eyes rather than smelling his enticing body. As was typical with Randy, she saw no deceit in him, only sincerity. He held her gaze, unwavering, and she couldn't help wondering what he was thinking about right now. Was he trying to read her thoughts?

"Really. You didn't."

Maybe she hadn't done anything obvious, but she had to make sure she hadn't propositioned him. "So I not do something... how you say... embarrass?"

He hesitated at her directness. Not a good sign.

Slapping her hand over her mouth, she asked through her fingers, "I tries something with you?"

After several seconds, he spoke, his smile very tender and sincere. "You were fine, Jovana. Don't worry. There is nothing to forgive."

Without intending to, her attention fixed on his mouth. His lips looked so kissable.

Her heart pumped faster like she'd just run to the top of a hill. Her breathing grew shallow. It made no sense to want to kiss Randy. She liked Kurt, not Randy. In fact, she was pretty sure she had a reason to be mad at Randy.

Then it struck her like a punch once again. He'd seen her naked.

Randy's tender smile faded. "Why are you looking at me like that?"

Her eyes narrowed from the memory and she fisted her hands on her waist. "I just remember you see me *gol*, with no clothes. You see my *pazuva*. Why you do this?"

"*Pazuva*?"

"My breasts!"

His gaze traveled the length of her and his neck turned red. "That was an accident. You started undressing--"

She gasped. Had she taken her clothes off? She wished she could remember the details. "I thought you say I tries nothing with you."

"You didn't try anything. You were peeling your sweaty clothes off because you were shivering. So I covered you with a sheet and brought you in the other room to change the wet sheets. When I returned you'd moved and the sheets that were covering you fell off."

Frowning, she tried to project skepticism in her gaze. If he was lying she'd know it.

"I'm not lying, Jovana. I had nothing to do with them coming off. I tried to give you some dignity by putting the sheet on you. I swear I didn't try to see you without your clothes on."

Tears formed in her eyes. He'd found her so repugnant he'd covered her up. He didn't want to see her naked. While she should be glad he tried to preserve her modesty, it saddened her at the same time. Why did she care? As a Christian she knew that was not the right way to be thinking about a man who was not her husband. She should thank him, not want to weep over his disclosure. "I think I understand. Is good you not want to see my body."

Randy peered from the corner of his eye and offered an amused grin. "You understand nothing."

Chapter Ten

Randy was glad to finally return to work. Only two more days at his apartment, and then he'd attend Bojan and Laney's wedding. After that he'd be right back with Jovana and staying at Laney's house. He looked forward to it and dreaded it at the same time.

He'd done some serious praying and studying God's word about self-control. If there was ever a time he needed to keep his flesh in subjection to the spirit, it was now.

Shep greeted Randy with a surprised smile. "So the boss has decided to join the living?"

"Yeah. I don't ever want to feel that sick again."

He popped Randy's bicep. "Looks like you lost some weight."

"Yeah, but that won't last long. Not with the wedding coming up. I always eat too much at receptions. There's just something about marriage that makes me hungry."

"Duh." Shep laughed.

Randy realized what he'd implied. "Um, I didn't mean it that way. But I guess that's true, too."

"Yeah, I was married before." Shep rubbed his chin and smirked. "It was nice while it lasted."

He had a hard time picturing his employee as a married man. "What happened?"

"I joined the service. While I was stationed overseas my wife started sleeping with my best friend. I wanted to kill the sonofa--"

"Whoa! I don't blame you at all. Did you confront him?"

"Nope. I did better than that. I picked up my things when she wasn't home and filed for a divorce. I didn't want to give her the satisfaction of seeing me hurt, so I walked away from our marriage like it didn't mean a thing."

"I don't think I could do that."

"Trust me. Given the right circumstances, you probably could."

"But I thought you said you had a woman now."

"I do. But we're not married. We just shack up."

Randy thought about the man who came by to see Jovana. "Has that guy been around lately? You know the customer who likes to hang out and flirt with Jovana?"

"Nope. Haven't seen him. Not since the day he came by and drove her home."

"Good. Maybe we've seen the last of him."

"Maybe. Is Jovana coming in today?"

"Nope. I gave her the next few days off before the wedding. She needs to get her strength back. She lost a few pounds and was still pretty weak when I left her this morning."

Shep gasped like a girl, his eyes wide and obviously mocking. "You slept with her?"

Randy shot him a heated look. "Why would you say that?"

He smirked. "I dunno. You said she was weak when you left her this morning. It sounded to me like you'd slept with her."

"I don't sleep around."

His employee snickered. "Oh, that's right. You're one of those moral Bible thumping guys."

"Hey, have I ever tried to shove the Bible at you?"

"Nope. But I know enough already." Shep grinned. "I'm an ex-con. Had me one of those jailhouse conversions."

"You go to church?" Randy's brows shot up.

"Sometimes." Shep laughed as he turned to leave. "Be back in a minute. I need a smoke."

He watched as his employee left the kitchen and slipped out back. That man was such a mystery that half the time he thought he could trust him and at other times he could swear he was up to no good. He couldn't prove it, but he had a bad feeling. Something wasn't right.

*****

Jovana finished applying her make-up and headed downstairs. The garage door opened. Heavy footsteps echoing in the house made her hesitate. She peered down the hallway and found her brother strolling in her direction at near-lightening speed.

"Jovanichka!" he shouted in Macedonian, "Praise God! You are finally well!"

His charming smile made her pause long enough for him to tackle her with one of his famous big brother bone-crushing hugs. He spun her around and finally set her on her feet, but refused to let go.

She couldn't help laughing even though the world spun mercilessly. If he hadn't been holding her she would've fallen limp on the floor like a rag doll.

"Let go of me! You are going to break my ribs!" she replied in her native tongue.

Bojan abruptly sobered and released her, nearly knocking her off balance. "You are much too thin. I should not be able to feel your ribs. I am worried for you."

"There is no need to worry. I have been thinner than this, beloved brother."

"Do not remind me. When I think of what Georg did to you I want to hunt him down and kill him with my bare hands. He is an evil man."

It wasn't until a tear slipped from her eye that she realized she cried. "The terror of my past life is over. You must forgive him. We all must forgive him."

Boki looked at her from the corner of his eye and huffed. "You are more righteous than I am."

A brief flashback from the days when Georg had forced her to sell herself on the streets zipped through her mind. Would the sick memories never cease? She nearly doubled over from the onslaught of emotional pain.

"Have I hurt you?" Boki touched her arm, then her cheek. The sympathy in his eyes strengthened her resolve to be strong in spite of the pain resurfacing from the flashback.

Several more tears slipped from her eyes. "It is only because of Christ that I have any righteousness at all, dear brother."

"That is true of us all after we've accepted Christ."

She touched the area over her heart. "I understand His grace. You see, I was the woman thrown at the feet of Jesus, the one caught in adultery. Jesus forgave me when I prayed to receive His grace and forgiveness. He told me to go and sin no more. I had forgotten this until I read the gospel this morning before breakfast. It was difficult because my English is not good, but I understood most of it."

"This is wonderful news! I must get you a Bible in our own language."

"You have done enough for me already. I deserve no more. Not after I got drunk the other night and embarrassed you. I was wrong and I am sorry if I hurt you."

"Of course I forgive you. Have you forgiven yourself for your past sins with Georg?"

Biting her lip, she wondered how much she should reveal. Somehow it felt right to tell him the truth, so she hit him with the worst part first. "Georg prostituted me in Skopje for drugs."

The look on Boki's face made her wonder if she made a mistake. He groaned and ran both hands through his hair, the look of torment in his eyes making her cry all over again. "God, forgive me! I did not do enough to save you."

Her heart clenched at the grief on her brother's face and the tears streaming down his cheeks. He blamed himself, but it was not his fault. "No, brother, you tried. I was rebellious and stupid. It was my mistake to leave our home, not yours."

"Oh, Jovanichka. You were so young and I was so selfish to be angry with you and give up looking. My heart is hurting for all you have gone through." He grabbed her and pulled her to him again, but this time she let him squeeze as hard as he needed to.

"Thank you for all you have done. You have saved me by bringing me to this country. If he is alive somewhere -- though I hope he is dead -- he cannot find me here. That is enough for me."

Her brother released her and wiped his eyes with his palms. He pulled in a slow, deep breath. "You are right. I do not want to hurt you further by acting this way. I am just so glad you are safe now and that you are here with me."

"Thank you for your many kindnesses."

"You are very welcome. Are you going to be ready for the wedding?"

"My dress is too loose, but Laney bought me two gallons of ice cream and insisted I eat at least one of them in the next two days. This should help. Just looking at ice cream makes me gain weight."

"Good. I am so excited." His eyes gleamed. "In just a few days I will be on my way to Paris with my beautiful new bride. We can finally live together as husband and wife."

Jovana giggled. She was so happy for her brother. He was the perfect match for Laney. Seeing them together over the past month proved it. "You look silly with that lovesick sparkle in your eyes."

"It is something in your eyes that I long to see, my Jovanichka. Is there a chance that someday you will find happiness too?"

She thought about Kurt and smiled. There was always a chance, but she couldn't say for sure. "I hope so. But I do not know. I am very rusty when it comes to dating. I don't know any of the social rules. I have no experience with men other than what Georg put me through."

"You need a kind man. Someone who will protect you. Someone like--"

"Do not even suggest it!" She shoved her hand toward him, flatting her palm against his chest. "Though your heart is in the right place, you do not know what is best for me."

"That is true." Boki stuffed his hands in his pockets and sighed. "But God does know what is best. I will pray until he brings the right man your way. Will you agree to pray for this, too?"

Her thoughts shifted to Kurt and she forgot part of what her brother had said. "Pray for what?"

"That God will send the right man to you that would be your future husband."

Her eyes burned with unexpected tears as shame washed over her. No one would want to marry her. Not if they knew about her life with Georg.

"Why do you look like you are going to cry?"

"I do not believe a man would accept my past."

"That is not true. The moment you accepted Christ as your savior He gave you new heart, a new life in Him. That changes everything."

"This is true, but the past is always with me, Boki. I wish I could see it some other way."

"Then I must pray for this, too. I will pray that God will show you what a treasure you are and how He has made you clean. You must build your life on this foundation of truth, sister. It is your only hope at future happiness."

She knew he was right, but a part of her still doubted that someone good and honest -- someone like her boss -- would want to marry her. Now someone like Kurt might see past her mistakes. But a good man like Randy Strong? She couldn't imagine him marrying an ex-prostitute. He deserved someone better.

Bojan continued to watch her, no doubt expecting a verbal commitment on her part. She would try to live her life according to the truth no matter how hard it seemed. Boki deserved this much.

"Okay, *bratko*. For you I will do this."

He kissed her cheeks and held her face, peering into her eyes with such intensity it made her squirm inside. Could he see that she was still unsure?

"Thank you, *sestra*." He released her face and smiled wide. "Now let's eat some ice cream and fatten you up for my big day."

Chapter Eleven

Randy checked the ledger a second time, but things still didn't add up. Plus, he couldn't find the green order slips anywhere. The restaurant only made half as much money as they did the week before when he was at *The Diner* overseeing the register.

He decided to ask Shep about his concerns and watch his reaction closely. Though Shep worked in the kitchen, Randy had made him responsible for the till because prior to going to prison he worked as an assistant manager at an upscale restaurant in Tucson. The man knew how to cash out properly.

He carried the accounting book with him into the kitchen. Shep wasn't there as expected, but the back door was cracked open. He found his employee outside talking with the same rough-looking man again, the one with the tattoos all over his arms.

"See ya round." Tattoo man knuckle punched Shep and nodded at Randy.

His employee turned to face him as his friend walked away. "You need something, boss?"

For several long seconds Randy pressed his lips together so he would think before he said something sarcastic, but he ended up being snarky anyway. "I think you need something. You need to quit smoking. You spend more time out here than you do inside working."

"Hey, I only take a break when we're slow, like now." He flicked his cigarette stub onto the concrete and ground out the butt. He followed Randy inside. "We both know this isn't about my nicotine addiction. What's up?"

Randy grabbed the book, stuck it under Shep's nose, and showed him the totals for the past five days. "Looks like we were slow the entire time I was out sick. Why is that?"

"I don't know. The economy maybe?" His employee shrugged, his face giving nothing away. "Plus a lot of people have the flu right now."

"I can't deny that." Randy rubbed his chin, still trying to get used to the beginnings of the beard that Jovana had told him looked handsome.

"You know how Jovana attracts the male customers. Things slowed down a lot when people saw she was out." The gleam in Shep's eye irritated Randy, but he caught a hint of anxiety.

Maybe he was on to something. "You have a problem with drugs?"

Shep rolled his eyes. "I have to do those piss tests every week. I may be an ex-con, but I'm not stupid. I've been clean for almost two years."

Randy wasn't stupid either. He knew people could cheat on those tests. "So who is that thug who keeps coming by here? If he's not a dealer, how do you know him?"

Randy watched for any sign that he might be lying.

His employee stared above Randy's head, his eyes glancing off to the side. He coughed and shifted his feet. "We met in prison. He's my bookie."

A gambling addiction would certainly explain why the till would be short.

"But I don't bet on much these days." Shep stared directly into Randy's eyes, a sure sign that he lied. "Just an occasional horse race or something like that. I've been winning pretty good lately."

Randy sniffed. "So it's possible you borrowed from the till to cover your bets, right? I couldn't find the order slips anywhere. I've gotta have them to balance the books."

Scowling, his employee responded with tight lips. "Are you saying you think I've been skimming from the cash box? You accusing me?"

"Nope. Just asking if you borrowed some and intended to pay it back. That's an innocent question, don't you think?"

"I ain't been ripping you off, but if it makes you feel better, I just won a hundred bucks. Take it."

"If you haven't done anything wrong why are you parting with your money so easily?" Randy raised his brows. "Just tell me where I can find the order slips and I'll back off."

"I didn't know that you needed them. I threw them out."

"How convenient." He clenched the book tighter. Bojan was not going to like this.

"I'm sorry, man. We never kept the slips where I used to work. Everything was on the computer. So I tossed them. You never told me I had to keep them." The expression on his face told him that either Shep was a great actor, or he really didn't know. He had to give him the benefit of the doubt until he found out otherwise.

"You're right. I didn't give you adequate instructions. But if I find out you're lying--"

"I'm not. Now please get off my back." He shoved the bill in Randy's face. "Take this."

Randy took it, rolled it up like a tube, and then gave it back to him. "Go buy yourself some nicotine patches and do your lungs a favor."

The moment Randy finished slapping the rolled bill into Shep's hand, Bojan walked in to the kitchen. Even though he'd done nothing wrong, Randy's throat tightened from seeing his boss unexpectedly.

"What is this? You give money to Shep? Is against rules. No lend money. Remember this."

Shep smirked and said flippantly, "I was just showing him the bill. Can you believe he's never seen a hundred before? You need to pay him more."

Randy scowled as Shep grabbed his car keys and slipped out back. The man made him sound like a complete idiot.

Bojan grinned. "Is this pulling leg by me? He jokes, yes? I know this is not true."

"He's full of it, but you already knew that. He was trying to give me his money so I gave it back to him. Nothing more than that."

"Why he haves large bills? He works for two jobs?"

"He *said* he bets money on horse races and wanted me to see his recent winnings."

"Ah. Is not good for gamble money away on horses." Bojan rubbed his forehead. "But is not why I come for talk to you. You have few minutes. Is this okay?"

Randy scanned the dining area. One waitress was cleaning up the last table and getting ready to leave. "Give me a sec to send the staff home and you'll have my undivided attention."

"Sound good for me. I wait." Bojan walked over to the waitress and greeted her.

Shep stepped back inside, grabbed his coat and saluted. "Forgot it. See you tomorrow."

With a disgusted sigh, Randy went to cash out the register and prayed they'd made a profit today. While business was slow, it wasn't slow enough to put them in the red.

Bojan patted the waitress on the back and locked the door behind her when she left.

Why did his boss want to talk to him in person? Had Jovana told him about what happened with her when she was sick? His hands trembled at the thought of Bojan's potential rage over that kind of disclosure. But his boss looked pretty relaxed, so he probably worried for nothing.

He'd just wait and see what Bojan had to say. No sense coming unglued over it.

Thirty minutes later he slid into the booth across from his boss and held his breath. Bojan had rubbed his hair enough that it stuck out on the side. He tended to muss his hair when he was stressed about something. Randy's stomach tightened as he wondered what had gotten his boss upset.

"You nervous about the wedding?" Randy hoped that bringing up Laney would put a smile on his boss's face.

Bojan grinned as predicted. "Is most exciting time for my life. Yes, I have nerves, but this is not why I see you today."

"Okay. So what's up?"

His boss's eyes filled. His nose flared and turned pink on the edges. Not good.

Randy touched his boss's arm. "You can talk to me."

"Is Jovana. I..."

"Is something wrong? Oh my God, is she hurt?"

"No, is not that. Is more like my heart breaks for her... pain. Does this make sense?"

"Why? Is she in trouble?"

Bojan grabbed a napkin and wiped his wet cheeks. "Her ex-boyfriend was evil man. He tore her heart inside. She does not feel she deserves love. I am only her brother. I cannot give this to her."

"What are you saying? I'm confused."

"She not trust man for love. I do not want to see her hurt again."

"That's something we both agree on." Randy swallowed hard. How much did Bojan know about his sister's torture by that sick gypsy? "What did she tell you?"

"Is very bad. I have hard time speaking words of such things. The abuse she tells about make me so angry I want to punch walls."

"I understand that." Randy cleared his throat and decided to make it easier on Bojan by bringing it up himself. "Did she tell you about being raped?"

The wide eyes staring back at him told him she hadn't disclosed that much.

"When has she tell you this?" Fresh tears slid down his boss's cheeks and he groaned.

"The night she was drunk she told me Georg raped her and his friends raped her. It sounded like a one time thing, but I never asked. I doubt she remembers even telling me."

Bojan ruffled his bangs and blew out a long breath, obviously trying to compose himself. "I am sorry I got emotions. I know is like a woman who cries, but this hurting of my *sestra* is so bad it makes me cry for long time. I feel no power to help. Nothing else can make me cry unless is tears for joy."

Randy felt tears of empathy welling in his eyes. Something about hearing his boss's broken heart tore him up. He coughed to try and conceal his emotion. "You can talk to me. I don't know what I can do to help, but I'm a good listener."

"*Blagodaram.*"

"*Molam*, my friend."

They sat in silence for several minutes. Bojan spoke first.

"Georg force Jovana to prostitute body for drugs. She know that Jesus gives her new heart and forgives sins, but I fear she will be tricked by sick man like Georg again. She say she does not deserve good man and no good man want to marry ex-prostitute."

"I don't understand what you're saying." Things were even worse than he thought. Poor Jovana had been through so much. "If Jesus forgave her, then why doesn't she just forgive herself?"

"I do not know. I wish I fix, but I am only her brother. She need safe man, a good man to restore trust. A man who kiss her and love her and keep her safe from evil men. I wish for you to do this. In name of Christ Jesus and love for my sister, please do this."

"Do what? Ask her to marry me?" Whoa. He liked her and he was attracted to her. He even got excited when he thought about kissing her, but marriage? That was way beyond anything he could imagine this early on.

"No, no. Not too soon. Maybe someday. For now just be friend and be safe man."

"I think I can do that." Whew. "It might be hard living in the same house with her, but I'll do my best to honor both her and God with my behavior."

"Is very good. I know I trust you for good reason. I would not mind so much if we some day are relatives from marriage. But is too much for thinking about right now. I just want Jovana for to heal and for you to help."

"I understand, I think." Boy, did he ever. The whole idea terrified him.

"She might try for doing things to test. You must kiss first, but other stuffs you must resist."

"What... other stuff?"

"I know girl once in college who a man rapes. After this she want sex from friend every day. She throws body at any man, even tries me. She hurt so much she not think about loving her own self."

"Are you saying Jovana is like this? That she might try to have sex with me?" Delicious tremors shot through him just saying the word. He had to force the image of her firm breasts from his mind.

"I do not believe so, but I cannot say for certain. She is baby Christian and she hurts much. She may do things to make no sense. Things from past. Things to make you... how you say... reject her? Is very important you be strong and do not allow her to hurt self like this girl I know from college."

Randy wanted Bojan to not worry and have a relaxed honeymoon, so he smiled wide and answered with more confidence than he really felt. "They don't call me Randy Strong for no reason. You have nothing to worry about."

Bojan exhaled with obvious relief. "Please do not tell her I say this. I worry she not speak to me if she knows I say stuffs to you about past. She feels much shame."

"Your secret is safe with me. I'll just tuck the info in the back of my head and make sure I am very careful around her to not give her the wrong idea about me. I'll make sure she is safe. You have my word on that."

"You are good friend." Bojan stood and gave Randy a side hug. He glanced at Randy from the corner of his eye. "You must remember to kiss first. You must be one who controls love, not her. I know this is hard for you but when time is right, you do this and keep her safe. Okay?"

"Sure. See you tomorrow night for the rehearsal dinner?"

"I for certain to be there. You must be there for walk Jovana down aisle." Bojan winked and strolled toward the front door of *The Diner*.

Randy offered a feeble grin and sat back down. His body tingled at the thought of seeing her tomorrow and walking her down the aisle even if it was for another man's wedding. He imagined kissing her with abandon. While he wanted to honor his boss's wishes, how would he explain it to her if she got upset? 'Oh, your brother wanted me to kiss you first so you'd know there are safe men in the world. Sorry you didn't enjoy it.' What a disaster that would be.

Maybe she would try to kiss him first. But wasn't that part of the problem Bojan was talking about? If she kissed him first she would just be expressing her pain. Hadn't she tried that already the night she kept offering her body to him? Now it all made sense. Everything she did with him while drunk was because of her past abuse. That must be what his boss was talking about. So far he'd passed the test with her, but that was because she'd been drinking. He just prayed he could resist if she was sober and in her right mind.

God help him, but something told him he was in way over his head with this promise. But it was too late to back out now. His boss was getting married and he needed peace of mind while he was on his honeymoon so he could enjoy his new bride. Randy determined he would do right by his boss even if things were very difficult.

He imagined her lips hovering over his and shivered. How would he say no to an offer like that? She was by far the most sensual female he'd ever known. He closed his eyes and tried again to block the image of her breasts from his mind. Why did he have to see her like that? It made resisting her that much more difficult. Like seeing his sister's friend when he was a young teen, the image was branded in his mind. But this time it was so recent it was still fresh in his memory.

The Scripture about taking every thought captive came to mind. He wondered if that particular Scripture included mental images. He prayed to God that it did. He needed all the help he could get.

Chapter Twelve

Jovana hung up the *telefon*, stunned. She had given Kurt the *grip*, flu and now he lay in the hospital dying? Isn't that what the nurse had said, that he'd been in intensive care on oxygen? Why was he being moved to another room? Were they moving him there to die? She couldn't even ask him because Kurt had had a nurse call her to give her his room number in case she wanted to visit.

Guilt made it difficult to breathe. She needed to see him and apologize for giving him *grip*. But how would she get to the hospital? Who could she trust to take her there? With her brother's wedding tomorrow, she didn't dare ask Laney who was working hard on last minute preparations. Plus, Laney had told her to stay home and rest, so there was no way she'd take her even if she wasn't busy. And with the rehearsal dinner tonight, that didn't leave her much time.

Her brother would probably rip the guy's oxygen mask right off his face if he recognized Kurt. So that left one person she could ask. *Randy.*

Hands trembling, she dialed *The Diner* and hoped to catch Randy before he left for the day. He answered after the first ring. "Hello?"

"Hi, Randy. Is me, Jovana."

"Well hello there! It's good to hear from you. How are you feeling?"

"Tired, but okay. I eat ice cream to help gain weight, but is not doing much good. You?"

"I'm doing better. Do you need something before I see you in a few hours?"

She swallowed hard. It was now or never. "Yes, I need drive to hospital to visit friend. Is only for few minutes. Then I must come back to house and dress for tonight."

"I think I can do that. Who is this friend? Do I know him?"

"Is Kurt, man who gives me yellow flowers." She winced, hoping he would not overreact like her brother tended to do.

"You sure you want me to meet him? I may want to rip his face off if he looks at you wrong."

A nervous giggle erupted from her. At least he was joking about it. He didn't sound mad. "Is not needed to worry. He is very sick and can do no harm." Her voice broke. "He may die."

"Wow, that sounds serious. Give me fifteen minutes and I'll be right there."

"Okay. I be ready."

He hung up and she relaxed immediately.

Randy was a good man. She would thank him later for his kindness. For now, she wanted to look her best for Kurt. He deserved a pretty smile and a friendly visit. If he died from the pneumonia she would be very sad. He was the first man to show a real interest in her since Georg. It was her fault he was sick. If she hadn't thrown up on him and let him get so close he would be well.

With a groan she brushed her hair until it shone, then put on her favorite earrings. She donned the same tee shirt she'd worn the day Kurt had taken her to the ghost town. He seemed to like it because he couldn't take his eyes off her. She loved that he found her attractive, but then again, he knew nothing about her past. She couldn't help wondering if knowing would change his interest in her.

No doubt Randy would find her repulsive if he knew she'd been raped and prostituted. She repulsed herself when she thought about it too long. Georg had ruined her life. If only she hadn't trusted him. She needed to guard her *srtse*, her heart from all men, even Kurt.

She couldn't risk being taken advantage of again. Hadn't Georg told her she was too trusting and too gullible? Even when he accused her of screwing around on him she still trusted him. In fact, she'd fought that much harder to please him. She should have left him back when she swore to him that he was her first and only *ljubov*, lover. He hadn't believed her and hit her for the first time.

From that point on their relationship soured. When he started doing drugs and prostituting her for money, any feelings she'd had left for him died. From that point on she merely fought to survive.

But enough of those depressing thoughts. She was going to cheer Kurt up if it killed her.

She applied a final touch of lip gloss and admired her reflection. Not bad.

The doorbell rang and she dropped the tube in the sink. Fishing it out, she dried it off and stuffed it in her purse. Hopefully Randy had brought her wallet with her green card and ID with him since she couldn't find it anywhere in Laney's house. She answered the door with a bright smile.

"Wow. You look stunning." Randy grinned and admired her from top to bottom.

Her heart fluttered like her baby had when it first moved, and she smiled back. "Thank you."

He'd kept his whiskers growing. She liked how that shadow of a beard looked on him, but forced the thought from her mind. She was supposed to be attracted to Kurt, not Randy.

"I brought your ID and papers." He handed over her wallet and she thanked him again.

She checked inside her wallet and then snapped it shut. Now she couldn't be deported if the Border Patrol checked Randy's car. What a relief.

"We go now?" She offered a bright smile.

"Of course." He bowed like a chauffer.

A giggle erupted from her. Randy always cracked her up with his chivalry.

He waited patiently as she locked the front door and walked to his car. He opened the door, making her feel once again like a princess. Too bad he was her boss and her brother's close friend or she might be interested in him. But even so, he was too kind. Sometimes she wanted to run screaming from him because he was so good to her. He was unlike any man she'd ever known.

And he smelled amazing, like spices and musk. But he kept staring at her. It was downright unnerving. "What? Why you look at me this way?"

Randy smiled at her, his eyes shining and full of trust and admiration. "Sorry. I don't mean to stare, but you're so beautiful it's hard not to."

"You crazy." She dismissed him with a flick of her wrist. "Hurry now. We waste time."

"Right." Randy shut her door and got in the driver's seat. "Buckle up."

She grinned and clipped her seatbelt in place. He was so funny. Just like her brother, he was always trying to make sure she was protected. At least when Randy did that it didn't irritate her.

Within minutes they pulled into the hospital parking lot. Her heart pulsed wildly at the thought of seeing Kurt again. What if he was angry with her for getting him sick? She hoped not.

Randy walked her to the sliding doors and was stopped by security. "No weapons allowed, sir. You need to hand it over to be locked up or take it out to your car."

While Randy talked to the security guard, Jovana slipped down the hallway looking for Kurt's room number. When she found it she hesitated for a moment, suddenly terrified of seeing him. The hospital scents reminded her of when she'd lost her baby in Macedonia and had to spend several days in recovery. That had to be what terrified her. It had to be the memories. Kurt had been kind to her.

Sucking in a deep breath, she entered his room.

Kurt's eyes lit up and he beckoned her over. An oxygen mask covered his face, but he pulled it off to the side. "Can I have a kiss?"

His voice sounded rough and breathless. She couldn't dash the hopeful look in his eyes, so she kissed his exposed cheek and brushed the wayward bangs away from his forehead like a mother doting on her child. "How you feeling?"

"Better now that you're here. I still feel like someone is sitting on my chest. If the people at work hadn't called an ambulance I'd be dead." The tenderness in Kurt's eyes melted her insides.

Tears welled up and threatened to spill over. "I am sorry I gives you flu. Forgive please?"

"Of course, honey. But the flu is only what started this mess. I'm in the hospital because I have double pneumonia." He reached for her hand and she allowed him to hold it.

"That sound very bad."

He stroked her knuckles. She liked the sensation and kissed his cheek again.

"It was bad, but I'm getting stronger every day. I just need to quit smoking or I'll aggravate my lungs while they are healing. Doc said I should be out in about a week. My lungs need to clear up more and I need to finish the full round of antibiotics before they will let me out of here."

She didn't understand some of what he said, but got the impression he was going to live because he said he'd be out in a week. "Is good news then?"

"Very good news. I can't wait to see you outside of this joint. Maybe I can take you to my apartment and we can really get to know each other better." He kissed her hand and winked.

She understood his meaning perfectly and needed him to know that she would not do those things. Not anymore. Not unless he was her husband. And she didn't know him well enough yet to decide if she even wanted that. "I do--"

"So this is Kurt? The guy who sent you flowers?" Randy strolled in and stood at the foot of Kurt's bed, his hands fisted on his hips.

Her pulse pounded and she trembled at the way he spoke with such authority. She'd hoped to finish her visit before he got there. "Yes. This is my... friend."

Randy frowned. "You know, I think I recognize you. You're the guy who kept coming to *The Diner* to flirt with my waitresses."

Kurt laughed, but then started choking as he caught his breath. "There is only one waitress who catches my eye." He looked at Jovana and squeezed her fingers. Hard.

She felt her cheeks heating and tried to release her hand, but he wouldn't relax his grip.

"Let go of her." Randy glanced down at her hand, still trapped in Kurt's.

"Not on your life. She's mine." Kurt shot flaming arrows at Randy and gently kissed her fingers. "Isn't that right, honey?"

"I... I... belong only to Jesus Christ." Jovana glanced at Randy and caught him glaring at Kurt. His pulse throbbed in his temple and she could practically feel his animosity. Kurt wasn't doing much better. In fact, he was squeezing her fingers so tightly she let out a yelp.

"I said let her go!" Randy moved toward the bed like he intended to intervene.

Kurt quickly released her hand and patted her on the butt. "Come see me again if you can."

Jovana was so stunned that Kurt had slapped her bottom that she was momentarily speechless. No good man had done that to her. Only men who paid to have sex with her. Men like Georg. But Kurt wasn't like him, or was he? She wanted to believe he cared and wasn't like the others.

"Come, Jovana. Let's get out of here." Randy practically spat the words as he touched her arm.

Stunned by their vicious exchange and hurt by the animosity she felt between them, Jovana merely nodded and followed Randy out of the room. She heard Kurt cussing under his breath, but didn't understand the words, just the sound of pure hatred in his voice. She shuddered and blocked the sound from her mind. Had she made a mistake coming to see him?

Randy grabbed her hand and led her to the car. "I can't believe you let him do that to you."

She stopped and blinked, swallowing hard. "Do what?"

"Put his hands on you, that's what. You're not his property."

Of course, she knew that. But the way Randy said it made her start shaking. Was he going to accuse her of being a whore like Georg used to do? To try and keep her from seeing her friends? No wonder Kurt was angry with him. He thought Randy was interfering, because he was.

That annoyed her even more than it hurt. "I know this," she hissed.

"Then don't let him do it. In fact, I forbid you to see him again."

She gasped, anger filling her veins. "You cannot forbid me. I am not a child."

"Your brother has placed me in charge of your safety. It's a job I take seriously."

"Is that all I am to you? A... a lousy... job?" His words hurt, but she wasn't sure why.

Randy turned from her and opened the trunk. "No, of course not, Jovana. You're a friend."

He picked up the gun and slipped it back into his empty shoulder holster. She shivered at the sight. "Why must you carry gun?"

Staring at her for a moment, he shut the trunk and turned back to face her. "It's a long story."

"So tell me." Her chin trembled.

"I will." His eyes softened. "But not until after the rehearsal dinner. Can you wait?"

She nodded, terrified from seeing the gun, and yet excited at the same time that he would tell her why he insisted on carrying a weapon. Georg used to carry a firearm in his belt. He said it was to protect her, but that made no sense since he often waved it in her face or pointed it at her head if she refused to meet his demands. It was an object he'd used to terrify her many times.

Would Randy threaten her with his gun? She didn't think so, but she'd been wrong before. At least Kurt didn't carry a weapon on his person.

Gentle Kurt, who probably lay in his bed right now thinking about her and wishing she had stayed longer to visit. What was she going to do about him? He obviously liked her. She found him attractive and wanted to like him back, but something made her hesitate. She wasn't sure if it was her heart or wanting to rebel against Randy that made her want to see Kurt again.

Without realizing how far she'd gone because she was so deep in thought, she noted that she'd gotten back into the car and was now heading back to Laney's *kukja*. Randy didn't say a word the entire drive, but she sensed he was thinking hard about what to do. While she was glad for the silence, she worried that he was still angry with her, too. What if he planned to tell Boki about her visit to see Kurt? That would be the worst thing he could do.

"Ron-dee?"

He turned for a moment, his half-grin making her breath catch.

"Yeah?"

"Please do not tell Boki about visit for seeing Kurt." She licked her lips and prayed he would understand how bad it would be if her brother knew.

He peered at her from the corner of his eye and sighed. "I won't tell him this time. He'd overreact and I want him to enjoy his wedding and honeymoon as much as you do. Just promise me that you'll stay away from Kurt. I don't have a good feeling about him."

She hated to make a promise she didn't want to keep, but in this case she didn't have a choice. She thought about how to answer truthfully and still get what she wanted. The perfect solution came to mind and she smiled. "If Kurt try to see me or call me I not answer phone. I refuse him, okay?"

"Sounds perfect." He patted her leg. "Thank you."

Warmth penetrated her thigh, but she tried to ignore the tingling sensation. She didn't want to change her mind because of Randy or anyone else.

Besides, she never promised him she wouldn't call Kurt first.

Chapter Thirteen

Kurt lay awake in bed all night feeling powerless to do anything as long as he was strapped to an IV pole and hooked up to oxygen. But his chest still hurt like an anvil sat on it, so he debated on whether to leave AMA or not. The last time he left the hospital against medical advice was back when he was married and his appendix had burst at work.

At the time, he could've sworn his wife was cheating on him, so he left early and his insurance refused to pay the bill. It took him two years to clean up his credit and he blamed his wife for that, of course. If she hadn't looked so eager to see him admitted to the hospital he wouldn't have suspected anything and left before he was ready for discharge.

But Jovana was different. He could see by the look in her eyes that she held some affection for him. He could also see that she found Randy's interference irritating. At first he thought she might be seeing Randy romantically on the side, but then realized she probably needed a ride to visit him and had no other choice but to ask him. He was her boss and from what he could tell, she wasn't his lover, though the way Randy looked at her made him suspect the man would make a move on her if he could.

Yeah, the guy was definitely jealous that Jovana liked him. Kurt's satisfied smile morphed into a chuckle, which led to a hearty laugh followed by a nauseating coughing fit that left him breathless. One more day to recuperate, then he'd try to get his doctor to release him from the hospital early.

How he longed to get a little taste of his precious honey pot. Just one more day in this hovel and he'd take that sweet thing to his place. Once she knew what he was really like when he wanted a woman, she'd be hooked. Yeah, she'd be his soon. It was just a matter of time.

*****

Randy hauled six pizzas into the reception hall, inhaling their scent through a crack in the warmers as he set them on the counter. His stomach growled and reminded him that he hadn't eaten since breakfast. Not that he could eat after that nauseating visit to the hospital.

As he followed Bojan back to his Hummer to get the rest of the food, he thought about his contact with his boss's sister earlier that afternoon. He wasn't sure he trusted her word when she'd promised to stay away from Kurt. When he'd driven her home earlier she'd refused to look at him.

Avoiding eye contact wasn't a sign of truthfulness. It usually meant the opposite.

Even after he'd dropped her off, she never looked back, which told him she was angry with him. That hurt, but at the same time she needed to know Kurt wasn't safe and that he'd do anything to protect her from him. The man was up to no good. Why couldn't she see that about him?

Then the truth nailed Randy like a kick in the shins and it hurt even worse. Her past drew her to a dangerous man like Kurt. That had to be what Bojan was trying to tell him. So how could he help her see this without offending her further? He had no clue, but he would do his best to find out.

For now, he just needed to make it through rehearsal. Any minute now he'd be walking her down the aisle in a mock representation of the event to take place tomorrow morning. He would also meet Jovana's parents for the first time that night. They'd had a last minute change of plans and decided to leave Bojan and Jovana's grandmother with a nurse so they wouldn't miss the wedding.

Randy didn't think Jovana even knew they were coming since she hadn't mentioned it. Bojan had said it was supposed to be a surprise, so he assumed she didn't know. Bojan expected them to arrive any minute and it was obvious by his pacing and constant fidgeting that he was nervous about seeing them. From what he understood, they had approved of his choice for a bride, though at first he said they were reluctant because she was not from their country.

Bojan thrust several six packs of soft drinks into his arms. "I see *rotidels*, parents." He pointed at a Cadillac. "I must greet and will introduce soon. Please bring pop to kitchen and place in ice. If you see Jovana, do not tell her they are here. I see you soon when I finish."

Randy watched as Bojan sprinted over to the car. His feet refused to move as he watched Bojan's parents exit their vehicle and wrap their son in a warm hug, kissing his cheeks, and then releasing him. His face lit like a Roman candle as he talked animatedly to them. His mother resembled Jovana in stature, but was a bit plump, probably due to her age.

He forced himself to turn away and complete his task. He missed his parents and wished they hadn't chosen to travel around the country in an RV when they retired. But they'd had him when they were in their early forties, so they deserved the time together at their age. It just made contacting them challenging, and he didn't like that. He had more contact with his sister, and even that was sporadic at best. As they'd grown older his family had grown apart.

Shaking off the melancholy thoughts, he cracked open the ice chests and tore off cans one at a time. Jovana approached him unexpectedly from behind.

"Can I help?"

Without thinking, he stood abruptly and nearly knocked her over. He grabbed her waist and released her the moment she looked steady on her feet. "I'm sorry. I wasn't expected anyone to be standing behind me. It threw me off guard."

She tilted her head slightly. "What means off guard?"

He forgot how hard it was for people who were learning English to understand slang. "It means you surprised me."

"Oh." She smiled shyly and reached for his hand. "Sorry."

Opening his mouth, he intended to apologize if he hurt her feelings but was interrupted by an onslaught of Macedonian conversation coming from the hallway.

Jovana's eyes filled with tears and she covered her mouth with her hands.

He couldn't help grinning. "Looks like someone you know is here."

She nodded, spilling the tears down her cheeks. "I miss them yet I scared for seeing them."

"Why?" He wanted to hold her and comfort her so badly.

Before she could answer him her parents barreled into the room where they stood. Her mother pulled Jovana into an excited hug. She paused with a worried look on her face and continued speaking in fluent Macedonian. It sounded like her mother was asking about her weight loss and was worried about her health. She grabbed Jovana's cheeks and spoke tenderly to her. Jovana nodded and more tears slid down her face as she asked about her grandmother. He started to feel like he was intruding on their private conversation and stepped back to leave the room.

Bojan caught his arm and pulled him off to the side. He spoke in English as he introduced them. "Randy, this my father. And this is manager of new restaurant, Randy Strong."

"Is pleasure to meet you Mr. Strong." Bojan's father looked a lot like Jovana, or rather she looked a lot like him, only prettier.

"Likewise, Mr. Trajkovski." He glanced over at Jovana who was now sobbing in her mother's arms.

"*Tatko*, this is man who stays with Jovana when Laney go with me on honeymoon to Paris."

His father scanned Randy from head to toe and asked Bojan in Macedonian. "Is he a good man? Will he protect your sister and not try anything with her? Two weeks is a long time to be alone."

Randy wanted him to know he understood, so he replied for Bojan in Macedonian. "I will not hurt her, sir. She is safe with me, I promise you this."

A satisfied smile covered Bojan's father's face. "You speak our language."

101

"Yes, though not fluently. Your daughter is doing very well learning English, but Bojan felt it best to have someone stay with her that she could communicate with if she was lonely or upset."

"Then I like this plan." His father patted Randy's arm, then paused and stared at him intensely. "But if you hurt my daughter I will make your life a living h--"

"*Tatko*! There is no need to threaten him." Bojan's face had turned red and his eyes seemed to apologize for his father's behavior.

"Does he know about her past? Her weakness?" Bojan's father kept his eyes fixed on Randy, probably to assess his reaction.

"I do." Randy decided again to answer directly. "Which is why I will be even more careful with her, sir. I do not want her to be taken advantage of by anyone either, including myself."

"Very well then. I will accept this plan." He turned and called over his wife.

She approached her husband, her daughter in tow. Jovana trembled and wiped her face, smearing her make-up. Whatever they had spoken of had upset her greatly. He'd have to ask Jovana later, when they were alone.

He spoke to his wife in his native tongue. "This is the man who stays with our daughter when we return to Macedonia. I have spoken with him and believe she will be well cared for and protected."

Jovana's mother eyed him skeptically. Apparently she didn't know that Randy understood their language because she said things that weren't very nice to her husband and adult children. "This man, I don't have a good feeling about him. He has this sneaky look they makes me wonder about his motives. He is, after all, a young man. And what man can resist such a beauty as my Jovanichka? Why is there not a woman who can stay with my daughter?"

Bojan answered with a smirk. "Because there is no one I know and trust who speaks our language as well as Randy does."

The stricken look on her face was priceless as she responded in Macedonian. "I apologize. I did not know you would understand me. I tend to speak without thinking sometimes. It's the protective mother in me, you see. My daughter is lucky to be alive. I just want to protect her."

"There is nothing to forgive. I understand completely." Randy continued to speak in their native tongue hoping to put them at ease. "So do I have your blessing?"

Jovana's mother sniffed. "I told my daughter that we will take her back to Macedonia with us if she cannot stay with a woman, but she refuses to come. She says she is not sure that Georg is dead and she is afraid he will find her if she returns home. I assured her that we will protect her but she is unwilling to listen. Boki, you try and talk some sense into your sister."

Bojan shrugged. "I cannot do this, Mother. I am going on my honeymoon. If she wants to stay here then I think she should be allowed to stay. She is an adult and can make her own decisions."

"Of course, I know this." His mother waved off his comment. "She is stubborn. Always has been. That was what got her in trouble before."

Jovana covered her face with her hands and stifled a sob. She was still trembling, apparently afraid that she would be forced to return with her parents. Either that or she was ashamed that her past had been mentioned. Given what Bojan had told her, he could see shame making her this upset.

Their father stared directly into Randy's eyes. "We will let her stay. But you must promise that you will let no harm come to her."

"I will promise this on my life."

Jovana broke away from her mother and moved Randy's vest away from his ribs so they could see his gun. "Look. He even has a gun. No one will touch me when Randy is around to protect me."

Randy refused to look at her as she pled for permission to stay and merely nodded his agreement. He didn't want her parents to see the concern and affection for her in his eyes.

It must have worked because he was greeted with a hearty hug by both parents before they released him and wandered upstairs to get ready for rehearsal. He glanced at the clock. They were scheduled to begin in ten minutes.

Jovana stood next to him still trembling and obviously trying to regain her composure. He handed her a napkin and she wiped her eyes. She glanced at it and groaned. "Make-up is all smears."

Randy hated seeing her so unsure of herself. He took the napkin from her and wiped gently under each eye until there were no more smears. "There, now you look as beautiful as ever."

The look in Jovana's eyes made him think of a lost child. Was that in response to his comment?

"Thank you," she whispered. "You are much too kind."

Her voice sounded strange, listless almost. It was as if she'd resigned herself to the fact that he was too kind to want her but she was unable to speak the words out loud. That was so not true, but he didn't dare say so. Not when she'd finally gotten control of her emotions.

"My pleasure." He tossed the napkin in the trash and offered her his hand.

She smiled shyly. "I can walk up stairs by myself."

As she proceeded ahead of him, he tried to not gawk at her shapely legs and notice how well the jeans fit her, but couldn't help appreciating the view. Her jeans were a bit loose, but not so much that he couldn't tell that she was all woman underneath. He stifled the urge to reach out and touch her bottom like Kurt had done earlier that day. Even though he thought he understood why, it still infuriated him that she'd let Kurt touch her body and she didn't correct him.

Halfway up the stairs she turned, and they suddenly and stood face to face because she was two steps above him. "You like me, Ron-dee? You like what you see?" Her hand moved to indicate her body the same way she had the night she'd had too much to drink.

"What? What kind of question is that?" He ruffled his bangs and swallowed hard, not wanting to lie, but not wanting to be entirely honest with her either.

She watched him for a moment, her eyes boring into his as she whispered, "You think I not see you, but I feel you eyes on me, touching me. You want these touches, yes?"

The way she spoke to him with such intense eyes and that sensual pout on her lips made him squirm. It was like her personality had shifted from a wounded young woman to a street hooker in a flash. He shoved his hands in his front pockets in case something stirred to life. Was she trying to tease him or test him? His heart raced and he scrambled for an appropriate answer to her question.

A grin formed on her lips and she released a sensual chuckle. "You must hide your excitement, yes? You do not want me to know, Ron-dee. But I know this. I feel it."

She reached her hand toward his jeans, but he caught it in time and held her back. He wanted to run down the stairs to get away from those eyes that searched his soul, but he couldn't move. She leaned closer but he turned his face away before her lips met his. Bojan had told him not to let her kiss him and he was determined to keep his promise. She had to be testing him.

He waited several moments, knowing that she watched him, but terrified to turn back and have their lips meet. He couldn't be sure that he would not succumb to the desire he felt stirring in him, so he spoke softly to her instead. "We need to go upstairs."

The only sound in the hallway at that moment was her rapid breathing. She sounded like she was either getting angry, or she might be upset enough to cry. He didn't want to look and find out.

Seconds later she ripped her arm from his hand and burst up the stairs. She left him alone on the steps, trembling and wondering what had just happened. Resisting those pouty Angelina Jolie lips was going to be the death of him. Something in his gut told him she tested him to see if she could trust him.

He'd heard before that abused children would often do that with foster parents. They would try to get their caretakers to strike out at them or touch them in a sexual manner. And it wasn't until they passed the test that those precious, wounded children would let their guard down and allow themselves to be loved. Was that what she was doing? It was the only thing that made sense.

If she needed him to be strong so she could trust him, he'd do it. He only had to pass this twisted test of hers.

Chapter Fourteen

Jovana avoided looking directly at Randy, but did sneak furtive glances when her brother and parents weren't looking so they wouldn't suspect anything was wrong. It seemed like every time she caught his eye he shot her a questioning look that said, "What are you trying to do to me?"

She didn't understand her own behavior. Something about Randy's kindness made her want to see him fall flat on his face, to show her that he was as weak as any other man. The only man she trusted in this world was her brother, because he understood a woman's heart. It was evidenced by the love he shared with his bride-to-be. Randy did not see her true heart any more than Kurt did. They both saw her beauty first, and it made her sick when she thought about it for too long.

At least with Kurt, she didn't sense that he expected anything in return. Sure he found her attractive. The feeling was mutual. But did he expect her to love him back from her heart? Something deep inside told her he'd love her for her body and nothing more. While that was not something she should be thinking about as a new Christian, part of her wanted to just give in and get it over with.

She missed *pravi ljubov,* making love even though she knew it was wrong to be doing that with a man when she wasn't married to him. If Georg hadn't been so into sex and hadn't trained her to respond so readily to any man who showed interest in her, she might have learned to control herself better. Now whenever she felt threatened emotionally, *pravi ljubov* was the first thing that came to mind. On impulse, she wanted to offer her body, to erect it like a wall between them, so they wouldn't want her heart. It was much safer and something she could control.

But oh how her heart ached to be loved with a steadfast, unwavering love that didn't seek its own way, its own gratification. This love could only come from God. She knew that, even though she struggled with accepting the truth and holding it close to her heart. She gave her life to Jesus less than a year ago and already some of the novelty had begun to fade. For some reason she didn't want to pray as often as she had in the past. She knew that Jesus had entered her heart, but right now it felt like he was far away and beyond her reach. Was it because she'd taken back the old Jovana when she began acting like her former self? The one Christ had died to save?

Conviction from knowing she'd hurt the Lord with her behavior made her heart twist. Why did she do the things she didn't want to do and didn't do the things she knew she should? She remembered reading the Bible with her *Baba* about six months ago and discussing that very thing.

The apostle Paul dealt with similar feelings and wrote about his struggles. She'd found strength knowing that she didn't suffer alone. Maybe she needed that again. After the rehearsal she would ask her brother to borrow his Macedonian Bible to study when he was on his honeymoon. Hopefully that would help her to keep her mind pure and cleansed from thoughts that reminded her of her old life and tempted her to respond in the former way.

As she helped everyone clean up after the rehearsal dinner, she approached Bojan and spoke in their native tongue. "I have a question for you, dear brother."

"I would do anything for you, sister. You know that."

The soft look in his eyes told her she was doing the right thing. "I want to borrow your Bible so I can read it while you are in Paris. Would that be okay?"

Tears filled Bojan's eyes. He dumped what he was holding in the garbage. He reached for her and hugged her tight. "I have longed for you to ask me this. Of course, I will let you read it."

"Thank you." She sighed and hugged him back.

He pushed her away from him until she could see the sorrow in his eyes. It was like he knew she'd been slipping away from God and was thankful that she tried to get back on track. "You are more than welcome, Jovanichka. Come. We must visit with *rotidels*. They must return to our *baba* right after the wedding reception tomorrow, so it may be a long time before we see them again."

Jovana nodded and took a cleansing breath. She needed to spend the precious time that she had left with her parents and enjoy them while they were still here. Once they were gone she could get back to worrying about Kurt and Randy. For now, she would focus on her family.

*****

The next morning as Randy straightened his red and black striped tie, he kept thinking about Jovana and her peculiar behavior last night. How would he resist her if she did that to him when they were alone? He couldn't imagine. Maybe he should talk to her after the reception so she would be clear about what he expected. Yes, that's what he'd do. He would tell her that it was not okay for her to keep making advances toward him and explain why it wasn't right for her to act that way. That should set a clear boundary for both of them.

Bojan adjusted his tux and glanced over at Randy as they stood in the foyer in position, waiting for the music to begin. "I sweat so bad I worry the ring slip from my finger. How do I calm and stop shaking like this?"

Randy pulled the red silk handkerchief from his pocket and offered it to his friend. "Here. Wipe your palms on this. Don't worry about the ring. That's what a best man is for."

"Of course, you are correct." He tossed the now-wet cloth back at Randy. "Please pray."

"I will. But don't worry. Once you see her coming down the aisle you'll forget everything else." He tried to fold the material and replace it the way he found it. When he finished, he glanced up.

A tender grin formed on Bojan's face. "I have longed for this day. Maybe a day comes in future when we do this again and I be you best man at wedding, yes?"

Randy's neck heated at the thought of marrying Bojan's sister, who was no doubt the woman his friend referred to. "Maybe. If God wills it."

The bridesmaids entered the foyer and lined up across from the groomsmen. Soft music began playing and Randy reached for Jovana's arm. She received him and he led her slowly down the aisle.

His skin felt tingly and warm where her hand tucked in the crook of his arm. She peered at him briefly and the apology in her eyes told him everything he needed to know. His shoulders relaxed and he allowed himself to be fully caught up into the wedding march and the ceremony soon to follow.

Since Laney's parents had died several years ago, Laney's neighbor walked her down the aisle. He was a kind elderly man who had taken Laney under his wing, along with his wife, when they found out she lived alone and had no family. They'd become close friends ever since.

As Laney and Bojan looked lovingly into each other's eyes and pledged their lives to each other, Randy saw there wasn't a dry eye in the sanctuary. Tears streamed down Jovana's cheeks, her parents' faces, and her neighbors. His chin began itching as he rubbed the salty tears from his newly trimmed beard. Exhaling a shaky breath, he wiped his eyes as the minister declared them husband and wife.

They prepared to exit following the bride and groom and Jovana shouted over the music, "That was most beautiful wedding vows I ever hear."

"Same with me." He glanced at her tenderly. "I see it made you cry, too."

She smiled and began walking down the aisle with her hand tucked in his arm, her head looking forward. "I like man who is not feared to show feelings for love."

"The feeling is mutual." Randy chuckled, but in case she didn't understand what he meant by mutual, he clarified in a stage whisper, "I feel the same way about you."

He glanced at her from the corner of his eye to check her reaction, but he couldn't read her face. He did notice her spine stiffening a bit when he replied, but wasn't sure what that meant. He decided to not try and guess, but to just let it go. He would wait and see how things played out at the reception and then he would talk to her about more personal matters, like her recent behavior toward him.

After what seemed like hours of the photographer rearranging their poses and snapping a million photos, they were finally cleared to go to the reception hall. He just wanted to sit down and eat something. He might also agree to dance if the mood struck him. A smile tugged at his lips when he though about slow dancing with Jovana. What fun that would be. But then again, if her parents were watching them and saw anything untoward happening, they may force her to return with them and that would be a disaster. On second thought, if Jovana wanted to dance, he would refuse her. He had to.

*****

Jovana's feet started tapping when the DJ played traditional Macedonian dance music. She wanted to glide to the beat with someone and looked over at Randy. He immediately glanced away from her. Maybe he didn't know how to *oro,* dance. The uncomfortable look on his face told her that asking him to join her would be a mistake. He would reject her and she didn't know if she would react in a reasonable manner if he did so in front of others. So she sat still and folded her hands.

Her father reached for her and asked, "Young lady, may I have this dance?"

She couldn't contain her joy at his request. Her father hadn't asked her to dance with him since she was a child attending her uncle's wedding. Of course, that was before Georg had gotten her hooked on drinking, and had stolen her from her family, ruining her life. Was this her father's way of helping her to see that he wanted the rift between them healed? Her father still didn't understand about her relationship with Jesus, but he tolerated her beliefs, so that was good enough for her.

"Yes, I would love to." As he led her to the dance floor she sensed Randy watching them. A quick glance from the corner of her eye told her that he was pleased. She had the sudden desire to impress him and decided she would dance like she had never danced before.

As she allowed her father to spin her around and guide her like Cinderella at the Prince's ball, she felt the years of separation leaving them and their hearts uniting. She felt like she'd become her father's innocent princess once again. Her imagination took over. She saw herself as the virgin bride-to-be dancing with her father at her wedding before he handed her over to her new husband.

In her mind's eye she saw herself dancing with Kurt and she allowed the music to guide her. Then Kurt disappeared and she found herself holding Randy. The bolt that shot through her heart terrified her and when the song ended she released her father. He kissed her hand

109

and returned to sit with her mother. No doubt the next song was too upbeat for him.

She felt the *pop muzika* pulsing through her veins as the heavy beats vibrated the dance floor and made her body tingle. People started dancing separately and many of the young people around her were getting into the song and shaking their arms and legs. Some of the beats sounded seductive and she swayed her hips in response. Her parents were so engrossed in talking to others that they were not watching her, but Randy's eyes followed her everywhere. She pretended not to notice but found herself dancing for him. She wanted him to see what she could do when she let the music take over.

An upbeat dance song that had been popular with the gypsies in Skopje started playing and she was transported back to the days when Georg had loved her. Before he'd convinced her to leave her family, and before he'd started abusing her. She remembered the power she'd felt when she'd made him breathless from wanting her; something she now regretted doing. But when she was younger the power had made her feel invincible.

She sensed a similar desire from Randy even though he sat across the *soba,* room. So she danced for him, beckoning him without words, and rotating her hips seductively until she saw him turning red and shifting in his seat. That was the reaction she wanted to see. She had him hooked.

Someone grabbed her from behind her shoulders and whispered harshly in Macedonian, "What are you doing?"

Her brother's voice brought her back to the present and made her breath catch. "I do not know what you ask. I was just dancing."

"You lie! You are trying to put Randy in the *ludnitsa* from your actions. Why are you doing this on my wedding day? I cannot go with my wife to Paris if I must protect you from yourself. You will not ruin your relationship with him by seducing him. You must promise me this or I will bring you to our parents right now and tell them to take you back with them to Skopje. Is this what you want?"

Not only did his voice shake, but his body trembled with emotion. She had never seen such barely contained anger from her brother and it scared her. "I... I... do not."

"Promise me this!" He practically yelled in her ear. Thankfully the music was loud enough to drown him out. She glanced over to where her parents sat and found them so engrossed in conversation that they had not noticed the drama taking place on the dance floor. She searched for the table where Randy had been sitting but saw that he was no longer there.

"Where is Ron-dee?"

"Probably splashing cold water on his face since he can't take a cold shower here. It was wrong for you to tease him like that. And in front of guests!"

She challenged him with her stare. "If he did not want me he would not respond."

He snorted. "If he did not want you he would not be a normal man."

A sly grin formed on her face. "You have a good point."

Bojan grunted his disgust. "I do not see this as a joking matter. Promise me that you will not play these games while I am in Paris, *sestra*. Promise me!"

"Okay. Okay. I promise." She searched for Laney and found her standing off to the side, probably waiting for Bojan to return. Her face contorted slightly, like she worried about what would happen next. How she hated to ruin their wedding day.

Guilt clogged her throat and she sucked in her tears, choosing to show restrained anger instead. "You can let go of me now, *bratko*."

"Of course." He gave her a gentle hug and then guided her off the dance floor, his voice almost patronizing. "I think you need to rest. Don't you agree?"

She glanced at Laney who stood chewing her lip. She hated to hurt such a kind woman.

"Yes, I must rest. May you have a blessed honeymoon."

Laney reached for her and gave her a hug. "I will be praying for you."

Her kindness made Jovana's eyes well with tears. "Thank you. I need many prayers."

Her sister-in-law released her and reached for Bojan's hand. A slow song now played and she led him to the dance floor. She watched them for a moment, but then decided to go outside and get some fresh air.

She found Randy in the parking lot pacing. She could tell he was praying because his lips moved and his head was tipped down, like he examined the concrete while he moved. Before he saw her standing outside she planned to slip back into the reception hall, but she hesitated too long.

"Jovana, I need to talk to you." His voice was firm, but not as angry as she had expected.

She wished she knew what he was thinking. He walked toward her at a brisk pace and she held her breath. She released it and nodded, stepping away from the door. She sat down.

He sat on the bench beside her. "What happened in there?"

Glancing at his eyes, she saw concern, but no desire in their depths. Just frustration. How should she answer him when she did not know the answer herself?

"I... I do not know why I act this way. The *musika*... I think it remind me of days when I go to *diskotekas,* so I start dances with no thinking first. Boki grabs me and tells me stop this."

"I saw him do that right before I left. Good grief, Jovana, I thought you were going to start pole dancing any minute. What has gotten into you?"

His words hurt because they were true, but the concern in his eyes made her want to talk to him. "I... I do not know. Sometimes I feel like old person takes over and forgets work Christ did for redemption and cleansing sins. I want to forget past, but it come back and haunt me like demon. I do not know how to fight it," she sobbed and grabbed his chest.

Randy stiffened so she held on tighter.

She leaned against him and cried, "When this happen, I hate me but I cannot stop."

He relaxed and patted her back. "I'm sorry this happens to you and I will do everything I can to help you break this pattern, but you can't do this to me when I'm staying at Laney's house. I'm strong, but not that strong. Do you understand me?"

For some reason that comment struck her as funny and she stopped crying. She pushed away from him, her lids heavy. "Randy *Strong* cannot resist?"

He groaned and moved away from her. "Stop doing that to me."

Her throat tightened. "Doing what?"

"You know doggone well what I mean."

"I... I do *not* understand." What did Laney's dogs being gone have to do with his question? She thought they were taking care of them. "What has Baby and Dude mean for what you say?"

"This has nothing to do with her dogs." He released an exasperated breath. "I mean stop pushing your body at me like you're trying to seduce me. I'm serious about this."

Horrified by his comment despite its accuracy, depression washed over her, settling like a heavy rain cloud. Unable to reply with reasonable words, she nodded. She hadn't told him about prostituting herself, but she didn't need to. No, she was doing a better job of it by simply showing him the way she used to be. Her own actions betrayed her and it made her sick.

Her heart ached from his rejection, yet she knew he was doing the honorable thing by trying to show her respect. Something she didn't deserve. So why was she trying to get him to fall into sin, to give in to her advances? It made no sense, yet she continued to do it despite common sense. "I am sorry. I will do best I can."

"Not just the best you can." He peered deep into her eyes and held her chin so she had to look at him. "You have to stop this. Totally stop."

She closed her eyes and exhaled. The direct eye contact was too overwhelming and made her heart pulse so hard it hurt. "I say I will tries best I can."

He sighed heavily and released her chin. "Why can't you just promise me you'll stop?"

Her eyes opened and she captured his gaze. Swallowing hard, she answered in a raspy voice, "Because I cannot make promise I cannot keep. I can only try best I can."

*****

The day after Jovana visited the hospital, she called his room. "Is this Kurt?"

His heart fluttered at the sound of her voice. "This is."

"I would like to see you but I cannot see you at hospital. I am sorry."

"That's okay, honey. As soon as I get out of here I will call you."

"No, I must call you. I promise to refuse calls you make but I did not promise to not call you."

She confused him with her broken English, but it sounded like she would call him instead. He could deal with that as long as she followed through. Plus, he knew her number and where she lived. "When did you want to see me?"

"As soon as possible. If you feel well."

Thinking about seeing her made him a bit breathless. Or it could still be the pneumonia. The doctor refused to let him go home for another three days. Maybe he could sneak out and come back to his room. He laughed at the ridiculousness of the thought, but entertained it anyway. "I can try. Do you want me to meet you outside tonight when everyone goes to bed?"

"That would be very nice." She giggled, and the sound warmed him to his toes.

"Okay, then. Is midnight too late?"

"No, midnight is perfect. Bye bye." She hung up.

He tried to call her back but got the answering machine. She must've called him from somewhere else. He heard music in the background, like she was at a bar. Maybe that was why she wanted to see him. She'd loosened up after a few drinks and wanted him to fulfill her every fantasy. She knew he was more than up to it, that little vixen, but he loved that she wanted to meet him for any reason. He would find a way to meet her, even if he had to take a cab.

As he watched the clock, he waited until the next shift finished their first rounds for the night. He pulled the IV from his wrist and the oxygen mask from his face. He could barely breathe, but determined to see her; he stepped over to his dresser and pulled out the jeans and tee shirt that he'd been wearing when they admitted him. The taxi would be arriving in thirty minutes and he needed to be ready. Dizziness assaulted him, but he leaned against the wall until the feeling passed.

He headed for the bathroom and closed the door. Without hesitating, he whipped off his gown and pulled on his street shirt. He started pulling on his underwear when a tap on the door made him choke in surprise.

"Are you okay in there?"

White spots filled his vision and he lost his balance. Before he could answer, the floor rose to greet him and his head hit the toilet on the way down. Everything went black.

Chapter Fifteen

Jovana waited by the windows in the dark and peered through the blinds. Still nicely styled because of the wedding, her hair looked better than usual, and despite her casual clothing, she looked beautiful enough to turn a man's head. Kurt would definitely notice and compliment her. Her stomach fluttered when she thought about him placing his mouth on hers the moment he saw her. She wondered what it would feel like, since he had not yet kissed her lips.

Glancing at the moon, she reflected on how her brother and Laney were probably landing in Paris right now, if they hadn't already arrived. She smiled and thought about how they would be enjoying their first night together as man and wife. Laney had once told her she'd waited for her wedding night. Tears welled in her eyes when she thought about how she had nothing like that to offer a man. Nothing that had not already been stolen from her.

Her parents had boarded a plane and headed back to Skopje early that afternoon as well. While the time she spent with them had been *simpatichen*, nice, it was much too short. She shivered and wrapped her arms around her waist, her vision blurring as a few tears slipped from her eyes. They had all left, making her feel lonely and wanting to see Kurt even more.

She sighed and glanced at her watch. It was well past midnight -- nearly one in the morning -- and she saw no sign of Kurt. Why would he tell her he was getting out of the hospital and that he was coming come see her tonight if he didn't mean it?

Maybe she had understood him wrong. Maybe he'd meant tomorrow night and she'd assumed that he meant tonight. With a sigh, she finally gave up waiting and decided to go to bed. She was tired and her feet hurt.

Thankfully Randy was in bed sleeping. They hadn't spoken since he brought her home. In fact, they hadn't even looked at each other. At least she didn't have to work tomorrow and could sleep in.

Yawning, she turned and slammed into Randy's solid form.

"Going somewhere?"

She screamed and hit his chest. "You scare me!"

"I didn't mean to scare you. I was just--" He thrust his hands out to block her blows.

"How long you stare?" She yelled and pointed at him. "Tell me this."

He pressed his lips together and she could see the anger simmering in his eyes.

His silence ticked her off even more. How dare he watch her! He was no different than Georg who locked her up and watched her every moment to make sure she wouldn't escape.

"How long?" Her chest heaved with emotion and her whole body trembled.

"A while." He folded his arms and a smug look covered his face. "What's with the purse? You look like you're waiting for someone."

"Is not you business." She avoided his eyes.

"Who were you waiting for?" He touched her chin. "Tell me."

Without thinking, she tried to slap his face, but ended up hitting his neck with the tips of her fingers because she was so much shorter than him. She needed more power behind her, so she swung hard and clocked him in the face with her purse. "You can not make me tell!"

He touched his cheek and backed away from her. "Hey! No need to get violent with me."

"I hate you stare. I... hate..." She broke down and started sobbing.

Georg used to watch her in the dark, waiting for her to go to sleep so he could get rough with her when she was too tired to protest. He didn't care that she was hurting. She wondered now if he'd ever cared. And while she knew she overreacted with Randy, she just snapped and responded like she had always wanted to with Georg, but didn't dare.

She could attack Randy, because he was safe. So why did she insist on hurting him?

His large hand rubbed her back and he whispered, "Shhh... It's okay. I'm not him, Jovana."

The manly scent from Randy's clothing and skin permeated her senses and she found herself relaxing against the heat of his body, which was strange because the scent of his cologne reminded her of Georg. Was that one of the reasons she acted so irrationally around him? But there was only good in Randy. She knew this and yet she resisted him. Why?

Because he was a man.

Something warm and tingly stirred in response to his gentle touch. A part of her wanted to see just how good a man he truly was. As she found herself calming, she snuggled against him and pressed her body as close as possible. The sensation of his hands running through her hair aroused her and suddenly she wanted to kiss him. Forget Kurt. She was lonely and Randy was here in the flesh. From what she could tell he seemed to want her. So why did he try to keep a respectable distance?

Would he keep resisting, or would he fall like everyone else? She needed him so badly to be strong for her. She needed his boundaries to bring her back to where they both should be. They were human, but they were also Christians and she needed to remember that.

But the intoxicating feel of his hand on her back and fingers running through her hair made everything dissolve until she wanted nothing more than for him to kiss her with such passion that it would leave her breathless. She wanted him to love her like she had never been loved before.

She tipped her face and he stopped rubbing her back like a father comforting his child. Her fingers grazed the stubble on his chin and she said in her sultriest voice, "Love me, Ron-dee."

He gazed down at her and she sensed his inner struggle. He sighed and closed his eyes, then he pulled her against him. She felt his mouth kissing the top of her head.

"Come on now. Let's go to sleep. It's been a long day."

Shocked at his refusal, she pulled away from him and decided to try again, her eyes searching his. "But I fear sleeping alone."

Randy stilled, and then suddenly burst out laughing. "That's a good one."

"I am serious." She didn't appreciate him mocking at her. "This is not funny."

"Laney told me that sometimes you get scared and she lets Dude and Baby sleep in your room so you won't have to sleep alone. I'll get their beds." He moved away from her and headed to the garage.

She didn't like being rebuffed, but at the same time felt pride swelling in her chest because of his response. He wasn't letting her manipulate him, and she liked it. But she wasn't done trying.

Dashing up the stairs, she went into the bathroom. She washed her face and brushed her teeth. Pulling an oversized tee shirt from her dresser, she slipped it on. She'd chosen the shorter one where the hem barely covered the tops of her thighs. She waited until she heard him coming down the hallway and the moment she sensed he'd entered her room, she bent over to pull the sheets down, knowing full well he'd get an impressive view of her g-string underwear. The light groan and click of her door told her she'd nailed the timing on that one. Restraining a giggle, she opened the door and peered into the hallway.

Randy looked like he was in the middle of praying again, his face now tinged red. The dogs had followed him up from the garage and circled his feet.

"You bring beds?" She blinked and tried to act innocent.

He offered a weak grin. "Got 'em right here."

"You put them on floor, please?"

Clearing his throat, he avoided her gaze. "Sure."

She watched as he settled the beds in the corner and snapped his fingers. The Chihuahuas obeyed and climbed in bed together. Seeing them tucking their chins into each other's bodies gave her a fantastic idea. Her mind raced with the things she could do to make his stay at Laney's home difficult. She climbed into bed, making sure Randy had seen her legs before she pulled the covers up.

"Night," she whispered.

He exhaled loudly. "Good night, Jovana."

Not at all tired, she waited until she thought Randy slept. Then she plotted her next move. She chuckled as she imagined his response to her next surprise. He would be shocked and wouldn't know what hit him. She slipped from under the covers and tiptoed down the hall. Listening for steady breathing, she finally sensed the change in his rhythm and launched her plan into motion.

*****

Randy was so exhausted he could barely see straight. At first he worried he'd never be able to sleep, but then the calmness of the night slowly pulled him in and his eyes grew heavy. Every muscle in his body relaxed and he curled up on his side, prepared to enjoy a blissful rest.

He began to dream that he stood in the middle of a park. He saw Jovana jogging toward him and reached out to capture her attention, but she ran past him as if she hadn't seen him. A few minutes later they were standing in the kitchen of *The Diner* and he did the same, but this time she accepted his hand and led him into the back room.

Draping her arms around his neck, she pushed him against the wall and closed the door so they were alone in the dark. She ran her hands over his chest and teased him. He shouldn't be dreaming this way, but savored the unconscious workings of his mind anyway. Strangely enough he felt his body responding to his dream as well. In fact, it was getting hot enough to make him moan.

Intense heat moved across his skin and he groaned. The sensation of a gentle hand running down his back and legs made him sigh. The hand moved and then stroked his inner thigh. He'd never had such a realistic dream before. It was so wonderfully sensual. Then the sensation abruptly ended.

He groaned and lay on his back hoping to feel that heady massaging again. He didn't have to wait long. A hand teased his belly and massaged the hair on his chest. His body stirred to the point it sought relief. He reached out and pulled the body closer. Warm lips covered his as slender legs straddled him. He jolted awake. This was no dream. Jovana had climbed on him.

He pushed her off and swore. "What the--"

"You mad at me, Ron-dee?" Her face flushed.

What the heck was he supposed to do now? "What are you doing in my bed?"

"I could not sleep."

He released an exasperated sigh. "You couldn't... Your brother never told me about this."

"About what?" She blinked, her eyes looking round and vulnerable.

It had to be a ruse. She was far from innocent.

"That you would climb in bed with me." As much as he enjoyed it, he hated it at the same time. Thankfully he'd worn underwear to bed. It had provided a barrier not normally there.

He could not allow her to do this to him. Wasn't that what Bojan had said? He had to be the one in control. Not her. This type of behavior would never end if he didn't stop it himself.

"He would not believe if you tell him this."

Randy rubbed his face and moved away from her. "I won't call and upset him on his honeymoon. I'll wait until he gets back. But you can't keep doing this to me, Jovana. It's not right."

Real tears spilled on to her cheeks. "You do not want me?"

He snorted and pulled the comforter over him to create more space between them. "I would have to be dead to not want you. But this is not how I will show a woman I love her."

Her mouth gaped. "You would not do this to woman you love?"

"Not unless she was my wife. Unlike you, I've saved myself for marriage."

She gasped and scooted away from him until she fell on the floor. She slowly stood, fresh tears welling in her eyes. "I am not good enough."

The look of devastation on her face made him revisit what he'd just said. He groaned. "I didn't mean it like it sounded."

Wiping her cheeks, she said, "Yes you did."

"I'm sorry. I know you couldn't help what happened to you. I--"

"How you know what happened to me?"

"I... uh." Oh, no, what was he supposed to do now that he'd let the truth slip out? Bojan had told him not to let Jovana know that he'd talked about her past.

"Did my *bratko* tell you about me? That I cannot count how many men I have slept with? That the numbers are too great?"

He winced. When she said it that way it sounded even worse. "Jovana. I'm sorry. I--"

"Do not speak. I understand. You do not want ex-prostitute for girlfriend or wife."

The story of Gomer and Hosea came to mind and he reached for her hand.

She moved away and snorted. "Why you touch me now? I am dirty woman."

"I wanted to tell you there's a story in the Bible -- in the book of Hosea -- where God tells one of his prophets to marry a prostitute. There is even a former prostitute in the lineage of Christ."

Jovana looked stunned. "You tells me truth?"

"Yes. I'll read it to you in the morning if you want me to."

She watched him for a moment, then slowly nodded. "I would like this."

"Good. Now please go sleep in your own bed. As a man, I hate putting you out, but as a Christian, I must. I want to help you heal, Jovana, but I can't do it if you act like this whenever you're with me. Do you understand?"

"I do. I had borrowed my *bratko's* Bible. I will read this book and ask God for help. Good night, Ron-dee."

"Good night." He swallowed hard as he watched her walk away. That was too close.

Right after church tomorrow he was going to the hardware store to purchase a lock to install on his door. As he lay on his bed and tried to sleep, his heart grieved for Jovana.

"Lord, teach me how to help her. I'm clueless."

Chapter Sixteen

Jovana dreamt about the Scriptures she'd read last night and imagined herself in Gomer's place. Would she be an unfaithful wife if someone good like Randy married her? The thought made her sick and she'd cried herself to sleep. Would she ever change? Wasn't it supposed to be easier to live right now that she had become a Christian? Would she always fight these memories or turn back to the very thing that had ruined her life?

Her hand rested on her stomach and she reminded herself that she was not fit to be a mother, let alone a good man's wife. If that were not true God would not have taken her baby from her at birth. At first she had been relieved that she would not have to raise a child who would always connect her to Georg. Then she just grieved. Some days she wondered if she would ever stop grieving.

A rap on her door jolted her out of her melancholy thoughts.

"Rise and shine. It's the Lord's day and we're going to church."

She groaned and rolled over. It seemed like she had finally rested only to get up again. With a sigh, she tossed the covers aside and entered the bathroom. As she turned on the shower she heard Randy whistle at the dogs and call them out of her room. He was probably taking them outside to do their thing and get a bite to eat. Her stomach growled and she closed the door.

Stripping the nightgown from her body and tossing that along with her underwear into the laundry, she paused and looked at herself in the mirror. She'd almost had him. Part of her was glad he was able to resist her, but the other part just wanted to feel loved. This was the only way she knew to relate to men because of what Georg had taught her. The day she turned fifteen Georg had convinced her to run away with him. Then he'd taught her what men and women do.

He was at least ten years older than she was, so at first she'd worshipped him. In fact, she'd trusted him so much that she allowed him to groom her to do whatever he wished. When she grew disillusioned with their relationship and tried to resist him, he'd beaten her and threatened her with a gun. For seven long years she'd lived under the worst conditions. Only this past year had she felt safe and only because he'd abandoned her and left her for dead. Then her brother introduced her to Christ.

So why did she keep thinking about the past and trying to repeat it? Why could she not focus on her new life? It was maddening.

She slipped into the shower and as the hot water washed over her, she thought about last night. Why had she not noticed how sexy Randy was before? It must be the new beard. She'd always been attracted to men with well-groomed facial hair. Ironically, Georg had been as hairless as a stereotypical Native American, while her father and uncles were just the opposite. The Trajkovski men were hairy creatures.

Yes, Randy was perfect in many ways. And now he hated her for trying to corrupt his goodness. It figured that she'd ruin their relationship before it started. She seemed to be good at that.

She turned off the shower and dried herself off. Maybe Randy would give her another chance. It couldn't hurt to try, right? With renewed energy she searched her closet for the sexiest clothes she could find. She didn't have many, but the ones she did have would make a clear statement. He would not be able to keep his eyes off her. Hopefully his hands would follow.

She slipped on a black strapless bra and pulled a semi-sheer top over it. Inside her closet she searched and finally chose a tight jean skirt that showed off her legs. She topped off the ensemble with spiked heels.

With a smile, she grabbed the hair dryer and styled her hair until she had it looking just right. She then applied foundation, eye liner, mascara, and an extra coat of lipstick. She had movie star good looks when she applied her make-up just right. In fact, other than yesterday she hadn't worn much make-up, so Randy might not even recognize her.

Grabbing a little black sweater and holding it over her shoulder, she slowly crept down the stairs like a cover model, making sure that Randy saw her pursing her lips like Marilyn Monroe before she reached the bottom step.

Randy's mouth gaped and he sputtered, "You can't go to church like that."

She paused. "Like what?"

He walked into the hall bathroom and grabbed a hand towel. He wet it and shoved it at her. "Wipe that crap off your face."

Stunned, she examined the moist cloth. "You want me to wash face?"

"Yes."

"You do not like how I look?" Her chin trembled. He thought she was ugly?

He leaned close and captured her gaze. "I think you look much more beautiful without all that paint on. When you are yourself, you... well, you're stunning. But this... this look is not you."

She looked at her reflection in the mirror and while she decided to do as he asked, she cried as she walked upstairs and entered her bathroom. Why did he not like the way she wore her make-up? Didn't all American men want their women to have movie star good looks? But maybe that wasn't the real issue. She had never been to an American church before. Maybe they were more conservative when they dressed for services and he didn't want her to embarrass herself. That had to be it.

After scrubbing her face clean and re-applying just a touch of mascara, a little bit of blush and lip gloss, she glanced in the mirror. This was how she normally looked, except she always pulled her hair into a ponytail for work. She didn't want to wear her hair up to church, so she kept it down. She also selected a modest dress and one inch heels and checked her reflection in the mirror. Now she looked like a normal woman, so how was she supposed to capture his attention this way? She shrugged and decided to go downstairs. This time she just walked down and left the strutting behind.

Randy smiled and whistled at her. "Now that is what I call sexy."

She laughed. "You joke me."

"No, I'm serious. I prefer a woman whose clothing is modest and whose face looks natural."

She grinned and approached him. "Then this is what you will see."

"Good." He smiled and touched her cheek, and then kissed her briefly on the lips.

Before she realized what had happened, it was over. Her throat knotted and she blinked back tears. Such a simple, kind expression of affection touched her deeply, and yet she didn't know how to respond. She hated not being in control of her emotions, but at the same time she wanted more of this gentleness that was so unfamiliar to her. Something told her that the time she'd be spending with Randy was going to be the longest, most frightening two weeks of her life.

She only hoped that she would not ruin whatever might have sparked in Randy's heart.

*****

Randy watched Jovana on and off as they sat together in church. He kept thinking about the story of Gomer the prostitute in the book of Hosea and how God had told the prophet to marry her. He couldn't get the story out of his mind. He felt like God was telling him that he was that man and she was Gomer. But it made no sense. He barely knew her and what he did know about her was beyond frightening for a man who had no sexual experience. How could he please a woman who had slept with hundreds of men? Did he even want to marry someone like that?

He glanced over at her and compassion filled his heart. She was like a delicate bird, all skittish and easily frightened as she looked around the room once the service ended. He tried to put her at ease by introducing her to only a few people and as soon as they could leave he took her to a small café in town. They sat across from each other and talked about a lot of things while they enjoyed fresh-brewed coffee and subs, but he avoided discussing the particulars of what had happened last night.

Every time he thought about her in his bed, he had to redirect his thoughts. She was the most sensual woman he'd ever known. They'd only made it through the first night and it was already driving him crazy to be alone in the house with her. He just wished that gypsy had not destroyed her confidence and caused her to become so hyper-sexualized. It made it more difficult for him to see her as a typical woman who just longed for love when she acted like a crazed nymphomaniac.

"How old were you when you ran away from home with that guy?"

She glanced up. "I leave home day I turn fifteen."

He whistled and gently touched her hand. "Man, you were so young."

Frowning, she said, "I knew nothing. He taught me things I did not want to know."

"How old was he?" Randy reached for his glass, but changed his mind.

"I never ask him. I think twenty-five... maybe more."

"Are you serious?" Randy's mouth gaped. "That frickin' pedophile!"

"I do not know what this means but I do not joke on serious things." She reached for her glass and took a long drink of water.

What was he supposed to say to that? "That means an adult who targets children. Or young teens. I'm so sorry."

"You say sorry many times. It not change what happened."

"You're right. I'm sorry I keep saying I'm sorry."

A confused look covered her face and she wrinkled her nose. "What you say makes no sense."

"I'm--"

"I know. You sorry. Do not say this again. Is past."

His mouth suddenly parched, he nodded and took a drink.

Silence lingered as they became lost in their own thoughts. He knew God had a plan for Jovana and he was determined to be part of that plan. He would help her by showing her that he could be trusted and that not all men were beasts. She knew her brother and father were good men, but she needed a Godly man for a husband.

He hoped to be that man despite her sordid past, but there was no way that would ever happen as long as she acted like the unredeemed Gomer. God had to work on her heart and bring her to the place where she was no longer insecure and she could see herself like God saw her. It would be tough waiting, but he didn't want to interfere with the work God intended to do in her heart.

As Randy watched her eat, he marveled at how beautiful she was. If she truly realized this about herself maybe she wouldn't throw herself at him or any other man like a cheap woman. She was precious in his sight as well as God's. How he wished she understood that.

She giggled and set her napkin down. "Why you looking at me like this?"

He laughed in response and asked, "Like what?"

She made gaga eyes at him and exaggerated it by crossing them.

Chuckling, he hesitated and cleared his throat, embarrassed that she'd noticed him staring at her, but wanting to tell her the truth about his thoughts. Maybe that would be the best place to start with their newly developing relationship. With honesty.

"I was just thinking about how beautiful you are."

Rolling her eyes, she laughed. "That is not all."

"Okay. I was also thinking about how precious you are in God's sight. Of how much He loves you just the way you are, without all of the make-up and sexy moves."

Her nostrils flared and she slapped his hand. "Do not make me cry here. I tire of crying."

He reached for her hand and locked onto her gaze. "But it's true. I think if you understood how precious you are to Him then maybe some of the things you're struggling with would go away."

She blinked. "How I do this? How do I see me as precious?"

"Through reading God's word. Hopefully through our friendship and... other things, of course."

"What other... things you speak of?"

His neck heated and he looked around as tears stung his eyes, embarrassed to be getting so emotional with her in such a public place. But since there was no one close enough to hear their conversation he decided to tell her what was on his heart and mind.

"Some day you are going to be married to a man who loves you for your heart. I believe God will use him to heal that wounded place inside of you that tries to hurt others and yourself. With this man you aren't going to have to prove yourself anymore. You will be safe."

She squeezed his hand, still clutching hers. "Is there such a man in this world?"

He swallowed hard and decided to lay it all out there. "Yeah, I think there is."

Turning her face away, she laughed and wiped the tears from her cheeks. "How you know this?"

Pulling her hands closer so that her knuckles grazed his lips, he whispered, "Because I believe that man... is me."

Chapter Seventeen

Jovana nibbled on her cuticle and stared at the phone while Randy brought the groceries into the kitchen. It was probably just Kurt calling again. So far whenever he'd called her Randy had been away from the house or out of the room. This time he walked up and stood right behind her.

"You debating what to do?"

She turned to face him. "What means debating?"

"Trying to decide if you should answer it." He crossed his arms and smiled down at her.

"No. I promise to not answer if he calls. I keep this promise."

The phone stopped ringing and her shoulders relaxed.

"Good." Randy rested his large hands on her waist and said, "I'm proud of you."

Her heart swelled and she blinked back tears. When was the last time a man had told her he was proud of her? She couldn't recall, but if anyone had, it was most likely her brother.

Randy stepped back and peered down at her. The tender expression he wore as he brushed the tears from her cheeks with his thumbs made her heart throb. She didn't know it was possible for a heart to do that until she felt it for the first time. Was this what love was supposed to feel like? Was it even possible to know real love after all that had happened in her short life?

She hoped so, but couldn't help being skeptical. "When you look at me like this, my heart makes funny feelings. I like them."

He grinned. "That's good to know. Have you ever felt that way before?"

Biting the inside of her cheek, she searched her memory. This throbbing was definitely a new thing. "I do not believe so. This feels like strange throb, but I do like this feeling."

"Good." He studied her for a moment, then slowly bent down to *bakni,* kiss her. The sensation of his lips on hers was so soft and gentle that it took her breath away. No man had ever kissed her before with such tenderness that she felt cherished. And while this gentleness scared her because it was so unfamiliar, she decided she wanted to feel it again and again.

On the rare occasion in the past that Georg had kissed her he would try to shove his tongue down her throat, and none of the men who paid him to use her had ever kissed her. That would have been too intimate. All they wanted her to do was pleasure them. Pleasuring her only occurred when they desired it to gratify themselves. When she thought about it she felt dirty, and used.

"Why are you frowning? Is it because I kissed you?"

She hadn't realized her thoughts had shown on her face. "No. I think about how men have not kissed me like this. What does this mean?"

"When I kiss you like this?" He repeated the *bakni*, kiss in a similar manner, but this time it contained unspoken passion and a promise for more. She had no idea so much could be said with a simple kiss.

Her eyes were probably dreamy, but she didn't care. "Yeah."

"So does that mean I'm your first?"

The startling reality of his statement made her wonder if everything with Randy would be a new experience for her. "This makes me a love virgin, yes?"

He tweaked the end of her nose and with sadness in his eyes, he smiled. "You're sweet."

She giggled. "You funny."

Stroking her cheek, he said, "The kind of kiss I gave you means you are precious. You are worth something to me. Do you understand what I'm saying?"

Her hands traveled across his waist as she hugged him and her hand bumped into his gun. "You say at wedding you will tell me why you must carry gun."

"I did, didn't I?"

"Uh huh." She pressed her cheek against his chest and closed her eyes. As predicted, he stroked her hair. She released a sigh, not caring if he heard.

His body stiffened. "I'll tell you later."

Peering up, she saw him frown. She didn't want to push it. "Okay, I wait."

He nudged her away from him. "How about we go to *The Diner* an hour earlier on Friday morning? I want time to check on Shep before we open."

"You concerns with Shep? Is he got problem?"

"The till was short every day that I was out sick. I just want to make sure it wasn't him skimming from the restaurant to pay for his gambling habit."

"He gambles money?" She followed Randy into the kitchen to help him put things away.

"He told me he gambled but said he didn't have a problem."

When she looked inside a paper sack she found what looked like a door lock. "What is this?"

Randy grabbed the small package and held it behind his back. "Nothing."

She lunged for it. "Let me see!"

He held it above his head. "Nope."

Jumping as high as she could, she still didn't come close to reaching it.

Though Randy seemed to be enjoying himself, she became frustrated. Plotting ways she could distract him, she spontaneously leaped into his arms and wrapped her thighs around his waist. He spun in circles like a dog chasing his tail.

While laughing hysterically, she squeezed her thighs tighter and reached over his head until her chest was in his face. He tickled her ribs, but was unable to peel her from his waist. She loved that she had the upper hand so she threatened in a sing-song voice, "Show me this or I not let go till you do."

He grinned wickedly and tossed the object above the cupboard so she'd have to climb on the counter and stand on her tiptoes to retrieve it.

"No fair!" She scrambled onto the counter and stood on her toes but couldn't come close to reaching it because he kept pulling her out of the way.

Now laughing so hard that her side hurt, she paused to catch her breath. When was the last time she'd had such fun? Not since she and Boki played hide and seek children.

That stark realization saddened her and in an instant her tears of laughter turned into sobs. She had missed out on so many normal things like simply playing for fun because she'd run away with Georg. And while Randy said he'd understood, he had no idea what she'd gone through and she doubted he would be able to handle the truth in all of its ugliness if she told him. In fact, he'd probably run screaming from her.

That notion made her want to pull out all the stops and test him again. Harder this time.

"You okay?" He touched her wet cheek.

She nodded and bit her lip seductively. "Make love to me, Ron-dee."

He blinked as if shocked at her sudden shift. "Jovana..."

"Please..." Lunging for his mouth, she tried to french kiss him. At the same time rubbed his crotch with her hand.

Randy's body responded instantly and he pushed her hand away. His voice sounded angry and a horrified look sparked in his eyes. "Why did you have to ruin it? You always ruin it!"

Her limbs froze. She didn't know what to say because she didn't understand it herself.

As she watched him reach above the cupboard and retrieve the thing they were wrestling over, she waited to see what he'd do next. Would he threaten her?

He showed her what he'd bought. "You see this? I hoped I wouldn't have to use it, but it looks like I will. It's a lock to keep you out of my room so I can get some sleep."

She swallowed hard. That hurt. He didn't feel safe with her in the house, like she was going to sexually assault him. Suddenly she found that ironic and she giggled. "You scared of me, Ron-dee?"

"It's not funny." His brows furrowed and he rubbed his face. "This is all messed up."

"To make love to me would not be so bad." She pouted and started unbuttoning her blouse.

He growled and looked away. After exhaling loudly, he announced, "I'm going to bed."

"But--" Her voice sounded whiny.

"Stay away from me, Jovana. I mean it!"

Her throat squeezed and she choked on the harshness filling his voice. What had she just done?

*****

Four days later Kurt was thrilled to finally break lose from the confines of the hospital. He rubbed the dent on his head where the blood had pooled and scabbed under his scalp, thankful he hadn't needed stitches. Unfortunately his accident had added another day to his internment because they'd had to run several tests 'just to be on the safe side'. That was a bunch of crap. They just wanted to bill his insurance for whatever they could get.

Stinking hospitals and doctors were so worried about being sued these days they'd wanted to make sure he'd had all the necessary diagnostic tests before they released him. He'd gotten a mild concussion, but nothing more, so he didn't see what the big deal was other than the humiliation from the fall. When he'd woken up in the bathroom three nights ago with his underwear around his ankles and two male staff looking down at him, he'd wanted to crawl out of the bathroom and take off running. He'd never been so embarrassed in his life.

If Jovana hadn't sounded so eager on the phone to see him he never would've done something as stupid as trying to sneak out to see her before he was well enough to leave. Now that he was being discharged he needed to find out what had happened to her. It was driving him crazy that she'd never returned any of his calls. Before he went home today he planned to pay her a surprise visit at *The Diner*. Hopefully he'd get there before they closed. Everything seemed to take longer than it should and it was frustrating the heck out of him.

The taxi company was the worse offender, taking way longer than he'd expected. He still needed to get home to change his clothes, shower, and grab his truck keys. He'd be pushing it, but he should be able to make it there before that vixen left for the day. If the stupid taxi didn't arrive soon, though, he'd start walking. No way would he miss seeing her. She hadn't bothered to return his calls and he needed to know why before he went nuts.

He didn't want to have to show her the error she'd made by ignoring him, but how else would she learn? And if she was truly sorry, he'd go easy on her -- this time. She would tell him the truth and never lie to him again.

He'd make sure of it.

Finishing the rest of his bottled water, he flipped it in the trash and checked his wallet to make sure he had the necessary cash to pay a driver. He found two twenties and four ones. It wasn't much, but it would cover it. He was about to start walking when he saw the AAA cab show up in the ER driveway. Though his pneumonia had cleared up, he was still a bit tired. Getting a good night's sleep in the hospital was nearly impossible.

The cabbie pulled up in the black sedan and Kurt opened the door.

"San Pedro Apartments, please. And hurry. I'm running late."

"You got it."

He sat down and sniffed the pit of his shirt. He definitely needed a shower and clean clothes. If he was going to spend some quality time with his gal today under the sheets he didn't want to smell like a septic tank. He shivered just thinking about having time alone with that hottie tonight. It'd been awhile since he'd had his manly needs taken care of. He wasn't going to let her slip through his fingers this time. Hopefully she'd come to his place willingly. He didn't want to have to force her to get it in his car because that could get messy and it was a lot more work.

The second the cab pulled up in the parking lot outside his building he pressed a twenty into the cabbie's hands and grabbed his stuff. As he unlocked the door to his apartment he noticed a foul odor coming from inside. It smelled like rotting flesh. Covering his nose with his tee shirt, he entered his place not knowing what he'd find.

He immediately noticed Fred didn't greet him. Had his cat somehow gotten out when the ambulance came to get him? He followed the scent into his bedroom and cringed. His sheets were stained with dried vomit and other bodily fluids. They would have to go to the Dumpster. He wouldn't even try to clean them. He checked the bathroom and saw that the cat food and water dish were completely empty. Panic squeezed his throat.

Fred, his long-haired Siamese cat had been with him since he'd married his wife, and while the old fart was getting ancient, he figured he still had a few years left in him. Since Kurt was in the hospital for over a week it meant no one had fed or watered his beloved Fred. His eyes now watered from more than the rotten stench.

He followed his nose to the shower and pushed the curtain aside. His cat lay on its side with its mouth open and resembled a stuffed leopard without the spots. The old boy looked stiff and dehydrated, but

Kurt didn't care about the smell anymore. He'd just lost his buddy and the pain ripping through his heart right now made him want to open a vein. Grabbing his cat, he held it against his chest and pressed his face against the fur between his ears. Old Fred loved having his ears scratched. How he'd miss the old guy.

Sniffing back the sorrow filling his eyes, he chided himself for being so sentimental. A few tears broke free and ran down his cheeks. How ironic that he'd cried for his cat, but had never shed a tear over his wife's death. But Fred had been a faithful friend and shouldn't have died. Who knows how many days the poor guy had waited for his master to return and care for him? Had he been in pain long? He sure hoped not, but thinking about his pet hurting and scared made his throat knot.

Cursing, he kicked the wall. He never would've gotten pneumonia if he hadn't taken Jovana out that day and caught the flu from the wench. He closed his eyes and lay his stiff cat gently on the bed, then wrapped it in the offensive sheets. He forced the pain down deep as he took the nasty bundle of sheets to the outdoor Dumpster.

Hating himself for putting his buddy in the trash like a sack of junk, he conceded that he couldn't afford to give him anything better. He swiped the tears from his eyes and gently shut the black lid. He couldn't see paying a lot of money to bury his pet even though he'd loved the old guy dearly. As he walked back to his apartment with his legs weighed down in grief, anger simmered deep inside. This was Jovana's fault.

Chapter Eighteen

Randy hated to avoid Jovana for days on end, but he didn't know how else to handle the sexual tension he felt around her. Maybe if she weren't so unpredictable they could enjoy some time together without her propositioning him. But she would never change her behavior if he didn't talk to her about his concerns. Plus after sharing his concerns with the Lord, he decided to start praying with her and not just for her. He glanced at her profile and his heart softened further. He was through being angry with her and refused to go another day without clearing the air.

As he drove her home after work on Thursday he decided that she was probably as lonely and miserable as he was. For the past three days they rode home together but each went their separate ways the moment they hit the door. She read her Macedonian Bible and studied English on the computer each night while he watched television or played video games. It was a pretty lonely existence and he'd had enough.

Tonight he'd try talking to her and see where it led. "You making dinner?"

Jovana gasped, her voice tinged with sarcasm, "He speaks!"

"Fine. I deserve that." While it had been days since they'd spoken, at least he'd kept his virginity in tact. That last time she'd tested him had been the worst trial yet.

She crossed her arms over her chest. "You cook."

"Okay, I will. But only if you promise to eat supper with me and talk about what's been going on with you lately. I want to understand so I can help."

"I give you chance to speak. But I not have to answer questions if I don't like them. Is deal?"

"Deal." He reached over to shake her hand as he drove.

She received his hand and kissed the center of his palm, smiling over at him with those sleepy brown eyes that made his heart leap. Why did she insist on teasing him every time he started to relax around her? He had to figure out a way to deal with her so it wouldn't make him nuts and he wouldn't fall into sin. Then again, if it was God's will for him to marry her some day, he could imagine the kind of fun wife a spontaneous and sensual woman like Jovana would be. He smiled as he imagined her greeting him at the door, but his thoughts slid downhill from there.

"You like this, Ron-dee?" She kissed his palm again, then started inserting his fingers in her mouth in such an erotic fashion that he almost ran off the road.

He whipped his hand away from her and tried to focus on his driving. His chest heaved as he fought the desire she'd drawn from him like a leech once again. "Will you stop that?"

"Stop what?" She grinned and winked. "You want me, Ron-dee. Do not fight this."

A growl erupted from him. He punched the steering wheel two times and swore. He pulled onto a small side street half a mile from the house and parked. He cut the engine and exhaled a disgusted sigh. "That's it. We're talking about this right now."

She unclipped her seatbelt and turned sideways. Her eyes rolled off to the side and she wouldn't look at him. She was acting like a petulant child and it made him want to spank her until she said she was sorry. Problem was, she'd probably give him a sultry smile and ask for more.

What was he going to do until Bojan and Laney returned home?

"Why do you keep pushing me? Are you trying to make me despise you?"

She darted a glance at him and shrugged. "Maybe."

"But why would you do that when I told you I wouldn't hurt you? Do you *want* me to go insane?"

A sigh escaped her lips. "No, Ron-dee. I do not wish to make you crazy for no reason. Maybe I believe you hurt me, too. I do not know why I do this to you. You are good man. You deserve good woman. Not woman like me."

"Oh, spare me." Randy frowned and pointed in her face. "I'm a grown man. If I want to pursue you, I will. If I don't, I won't. It's that simple."

She rubbed her forehead and sighed. "Is not simple for me. Is hard."

"Why, Jovana? Tell me why."

Her head tipped so he could only see her scalp. He waited for her to look up, but she didn't move for several minutes. Not sure if she was thinking or praying, he decided to give her a while longer to pull it together so they could finish their discussion.

He watched her breathing and noticed a few drops of water hitting her arm that she'd rested on her lap. She had to be crying. He hated that he made her cry so often, but what else could he do? They couldn't keep going like this and live in the same house without something going wrong.

"I cannot love you." Her voice was so soft he could barely hear her.

"What?"

She lifted her head and said through tears, "I cannot love you, Ron-dee. I do not know how to love good man. I do not know how to accept this love you offer. It scares me."

"Oh, honey..." He ached to touch her so he placed his hand on her cheek. She closed her eyes and remained so still she almost looked dead, except for the tears running down her cheeks.

Her lips begged to be kissed. He wasn't ready to give up just yet, so he leaned closer to her and waited to see if she'd pull away. When she allowed him to continue, he brushed his lips against hers, but she remained still and didn't respond. The salty taste on his lips made him want to weep for her pain, so he placed his hand on her other cheek and offered her another gentle kiss. This time her lips stirred beneath his, but only for a moment.

That was enough to keep him going, though, so he kissed her again and nudged her lips apart with his own. He sensed a gentle stirring in her soul, like something dormant and beautiful had awakened. He coaxed her soft mouth until it began to respond to his in kind. His tongue slipped between her lips and teased, just enough to let her know he wanted to give her more.

She tilted her head and parted her lips further. His tongue glided across hers until she sparked to life, and with a moan plunged her fingers into his hair. He tried to quell his excitement with slow, deliberate breaths, but was quickly becoming entrenched in their deep kissing.

He wanted to taste more of her, like a parched man seeing a drink, but he held back as his lips explored hers with gentle persuasion. She responded much like a novice who was eager to learn, and she focused totally on him. Thankfully her hands didn't stray from his hair because at any moment he thought he'd burst from the kissing alone. Anything more would be embarrassing because of his lack of experience. And though he wanted to learn everything about her, he knew they should stop. But knowing and doing were two different things.

A truck roared past and made him jump back. Who in their right mind would be driving fifty on an unpaved road with a speed limit of twenty-five? He strained to see the vehicle, but the dirt swirling behind the truck made it impossible to identify it. "That person's crazy."

Jovana smiled, her eyes closed. "Is wrong for me to enjoy so much."

"Wrong? To like kissing me?"

"Yes. Is like piece of heaven. I could kiss for hours."

He stroked her chin with his thumb. "Me, too." Leaning in for one more kiss, he released her and waited.

"I want for love you, Ron-dee. Please show me how."

Not sure if her comment implied more than just kissing, he cleared his throat and waited on the Lord to speak to him and tell him what to do. He didn't want to go off and do something he'd regret if it wasn't God's intention for his life. The only way to know was to be quiet before the Lord and wait. It didn't take long for the answer to come this time.

Marry her.

Randy swallowed hard. Had God just spoken to his heart? Shivering even though it was warm inside the car, he peered deep into Jovana's eyes to see if he could even say it. A love sweeter than anything he'd ever experience poured over him like fragrant oil. He wanted to share his life with her. He wanted her to know what true love was because he was discovering it with her now, despite how maddening and wonderfully crazy she acted toward him.

"Marry me, Jovana."

The little gasp that escaped her lips told him she hadn't planned on him asking. Sheesh, he hadn't planned on asking her either. But he'd learned from past mistakes that ignoring God's voice only led to disobedience and further heartache.

Her mouth remained opened, but no sound came out. It was as if she'd become suddenly mute. "Say something."

"Are... are you sure? This is what you want?"

"Very sure."

"Then I must pray. If I feel in my heart God agrees I will tell you. But I must say I do not like guns. I do not want man who carries gun or has guns in house. This remind me too much of Georg."

"He used to carry a gun?"

"Every day he takes it everywhere he go. My mother say when she calls me yesterday that she hears he gets murdered by another gypsy at drug party. She said neighbor tell her she think she sees picture of Georg in paper where people that die in Skopje make list."

"You think he's dead?"

She licked her lips. "I believe so. I do not have this feeling of... how you say... doom, now."

He offered a sad, teasing smile. "But if it's true then you'll have no reason to stay in Arizona."

A wide grin tugged at her mouth and she squeezed the hands she now held. "Something in my heart tell me I have much reasons for to stay. The most special reason is man with nice beard who kiss me like wonderful dessert of lips."

"Would you like another treat?"

"Yes, I do. Very much. Is wonderful feelings this makes in heart."

"Okay, but if this relationship of ours is going to work, you need to let me initiate everything."

"What means initiate?"

"That means I start everything, including kisses. You just respond. Can you do that?"

"I... I will try. Is difficult for me to do this, but I see how this help me change."

"Mmm hmmm. Let's see how well you do now." He leaned in for another amazing kiss. They engaged each other's mouths with tender abandon. Randy sank so deeply into the moment he forgot where they were... until something hard like a stone cracked his windshield. He jumped back and tried to catch the make and model of the vehicle that shot a rock from its tires because the driver was speeding. It looked like the same guy who had just peeled down the street at a dangerous speed not that long ago. Smoke and dirt spewed from behind the vehicle, once again obscuring their view.

Jovana bit her lip and glanced at the fresh crack in the windshield. "I am sorry. If we not stop here for talking, this not happen to you."

"That's the most ridiculous thing I've ever heard."

"You think is delivery truck? It comes down road from near Laney's house."

"Who knows?" Randy started the vehicle and steered onto the road that headed to Laney's place.

Jovana reached for Randy's hand. "Thanks much for beautiful day. The kisses make me feel like I deserve you love."

"That's because you do."

Randy hesitated a moment, but when he parked in Laney's garage he decided that maybe she was ready to hear his traumatic story about the robbery in Tucson and why he carried a gun. By the end of his very scaled-down version of the story Jovana reached over the hand rest and embraced him with tears filling her eyes.

"You understand pain. Is good to know. Maybe we help each other."

"I think that's why God brought us together. He sighed with contentment and wished for the peaceful moment to last forever. "If anything ever happened to you, I wouldn't be able to handle it."

Jovana smiled and snuggled against him. "*Fala,* thanks."

"*Molam,* you are welcome, sweetheart." After planting another brief kiss on her lips, he turned on the garage remote smiling stupidly at her while the door lowered. She flicked on the light and frowned as she examined something.

"Ron-dee? What you think is this?"

He glanced over to see what had captured her attention. Kurt's face flashed through his mind, but only briefly. "Looks like blood. Like someone hit the door *hard* with their knuckles. See the little dents?"

Her eyes widened. "Who would do this?"

"I don't know."

"You think maybe is Kurt? I have not calls back and this make him mad you think?

A sense of foreboding prickled his skin and he determined to never let her out of his site... even if it was the middle of the night.

But now he had to worry about how would he keep her in her own bed.

"I'm keeping my eye on you and moving your twin bed into my room until they return. I don't want to take any chances." He touched her cheek. "You're too precious to me."

She studied him for a moment. "You trust me in same room?"

"I'm going to have to." But how would he ever sleep?

*****

Jovana saw the worry in Randy's eyes and wanted to reassure him that she could behave, but what if that wasn't true? Sometimes she acted on impulse and surprised herself. "You and I must pray."

He heaved a sigh. "Including God in our plans certainly can't hurt."

She reached for his hands and they prayed for each other. Randy's words were so heartfelt she wanted him all the more. But could she be his wife? She'd have to check with God on that in the morning. Right now she just wanted to enjoy her evening with Randy. "Amen."

He went to the downstairs bathroom and she headed upstairs. After washing her face, brushing her teeth, and changing into an oversized tee shirt, she approached Randy. He had already pushed her frame into the other room and was arranging the mattresses when she stood behind him and wrapped her arms around his waist. She pressed her cheek into his muscular back and whispered, "Thank you."

He turned so they faced each other and he scanned her briefly. "Thanks for wearing a longer shirt to bed. What you wore the other night was mean."

She snickered and teased him. "Is same under shirt, just cover more of legs so you not get mad."

A laugh burst from him. "I would be more likely to go mad than get mad. Now stop telling me sexy things like that."

"Like what?" She blinked her eyes like she didn't know what he meant, but she did.

He nudged her gently toward her bed. "Climb under the covers before I'm tempted to peek."

Scampering over to the bed, she slipped under the sheets. With a grin, she teased, "Now is safe for you sleep, okay? I stay in this bed. I promise I will not do things... I hope."

She heard a muffled moan and suppressed a chuckle. He was so fun to play with. She could only imagine that things would get better if they did marry each other. As she prayed for wisdom, her eyes grew heavy and she fell fast asleep.

What seemed like a very short time later, she woke to the sound of Randy talking to himself in his sleep. She climbed out of bed and moved close enough to hear him.

His face contorted and he muttered, "I'm sorry, Mel. I'm so sorry. I tried to help, but I couldn't move. I tried." A moan escaped him and he choked on a sob. "Why?"

She watched him toss and turn, tears falling from his eyes. Hating to see him suffer from obvious distress, she nudged his arm. "Ron-dee. Wake up. You haves bad dream."

He sucked in a deep breath and opened his eyes. "What?"

"You get upset and cry in sleep. Some person Mel is hurt in you dream. Who is this?"

Randy rubbed his eyes and hesitated. "I often have this dream about the night of the attack. Most of the time I save her in my dream, but sometimes I'm too late."

"You love this Mel?"

"No, she just worked for me. Remember when I told you those bad men had robbed my restaurant? They hit me with a crowbar and knocked me out, but I could still hear them raping Mel. I couldn't move or open my eyes. The sound of her cries begging them to stop haunts my dreams." Randy wiped his wet cheeks. "Sorry to cry about it. I usually cope better than this."

She sat on the bed beside him. "You tired. I understand when sufferings is bad."

He looked at her like what she'd said made no sense. "You mentioned that. When you were sick with the flu you cried in your sleep about a baby. It sounded like you meant your child."

Tears flooded her eyes. "I pregnant by Georg two times. First time he find out and hit me and I lose child about three to four month in pregnancy. Second time is much worse."

"Not to be rude, but how did you know he was the father?"

"Is not hard to know, because first time he is only man with I have sex. He also make them wear... how you say... those things men put on for protect from disease?"

"Condoms?" His brows shot up and his face flushed so deep she could see it in the dim room.

"He worries for AIDS so he make them do this. He did not stop and wear them so he must be father. Does this make sense?"

"So you were pregnant twice?"

"May be more times but I not know if I miscarry. Many days I so drunk I did not care."

"It makes sense given what happened. I would probably do the same."

She sniffled and her nose began to run from crying. "He starve me and beat me and I lose baby when water break. I have baby born two months early, before is due. Now I do not know if body can have more babies. I scared for to ask."

His eyes softened and his kissed her forehead. "You deserve to be a mother, Jovana. If you have a strong enough marriage there is no reason you can't. Even if you have to adopt a child."

"What if God does not want this for me? He control life and death. Is not something I can do."

"That's true. But I know God has big plans for your life." He pulled her into a comforting hug. "I think being a mom is one of them."

She glanced up at him and sniffled. "You believe this for me?"

"With all my heart."

Her heart swelled from the sensation of being utterly loved. It had everything to do with Randy's kind words spoken sincerely and absolutely nothing to do with sexual feelings. She buried her face in his tee shirt, no doubt wetting it with tears and snot from her runny nose. Randy didn't seem to care.

She thought about going back to her own bed, but she didn't want to let go. Neither spoke and within minutes she heard Randy's breathing deepen and start to drag out. He sounded like he'd fallen back asleep. Not wanting to disturb him, she allowed herself to be held and joined him in slumber.

The morning came quickly and Randy woke first, startling her awake. "Jovana?"

"Yes?" She sat up and rubbed her eyes.

"I can't believe we actually slept in the same bed and didn't do anything. Is that a miracle, or what?" He kissed her cheek, then hugged her and sighed.

Something inside her stirred in response that was far from innocent. Now that she wasn't so tired she had the urge to teach him a few things about being a good lover. He said he'd never made love to a woman. It would be so easy to take him there. And once this sweet man was satisfied, he'd be hooked.

With her nose, she nuzzled his neck and released a sultry chuckle.

His breathing quickened and she knew that he hadn't missed her subtle seduction. "Jo..."

"Hmmm... ?" Her lips traveled up his neck and she worked her way toward his mouth.

"Um... Jo..." His voice sounded firmer this time.

"I do not know this Jo you speak of," she whispered as her mouth latched on to his and she slowly suckled his lips, one at a time. He moaned and turned his body to face her. His arousal pressed against her leg, which spurred her on.

As if suddenly realizing what he was doing with her, Randy pulled away. "Jovana, please! Don't ruin a good thing."

She frowned, though secretly she admired his willpower. "Is not ruins for us."

He rolled off the bed and turned away from her. "We can't keep doing this. No more touching or kissing when we're in the same bed. Please respect this, Jovana, and don't test me."

She couldn't see his expression but from the sound of his voice, she knew he meant business. "I promise. I know I say this before but I must promise." She knelt on the mattress and hugged him from behind, tears spilling from her eyes. "I cannot lose you, Ron-dee. Help me to be women you respect."

A deep sigh escaped him and he said softly, "I do respect you, Jovana. The problem is waiting for you. I can't have what isn't mine. Until you marry me, we have to control ourselves."

"Okay. Then we must marry so you are not unhappy to wait long time."

He turned to face her. "So I'm not unhappy? What about you?"

She shrugged. "You kind man. I please you. Is good enough, yes?"

"No. I need to know that you love me with your whole heart and you don't want anyone else. Unless this is true, we shouldn't get married. I don't even know if I can please you, which is why there must be love holding us together. It's a lifetime commitment that I take very seriously."

Smiling, she squeezed him tight and whispered in his ear. "Then we must start this new life."

Chapter Nineteen

Kurt was ready to strangle someone. By the time he'd arrived at *The Diner* it had already closed, so he drove to Jovana's home and nearly beat the door down, but she never answered. He was ready to fight with someone just to get some relief from the pressure building inside him. He grabbed some ice from the freezer and wrapped his hand with a towel to help reduce the swelling. As he relaxed in his chair and watched television, he downed a few beers to help numb the pain. Before he knew what happened he'd fallen asleep.

The next morning he woke before the sun had risen and he was still sitting in his chair. His stiff fingers had scabs forming over the cuts on his hand, but it was usable. Hopefully he hadn't left any dents on the door because if he had, Jovana would take one look at his hand and know he was the man who had nearly beaten it down. Regardless, he had every intention of seeing her this morning before she started her shift. He wanted her to know about his cat dying to see if she'd apologize.

He found a spot near the dumpsters on the far end of the parking lot and sat there for a moment. Within minutes someone showed up and opened the back door. Kurt recognized the guy as the cook. Someone he'd never seen before stood behind the guy and followed him inside. It almost looked like he had something poking in the cook's back, but it was so hard to tell with the dark sky and from such a distance.

About a minute later he heard a gunshot, which confirmed his suspicions. Kurt squeezed the steering wheel with his hands and debated what to do. Now rather than being angry with Jovana he was scared for her. She'd show up any minute and walk inside... to what? Would she get shot? Should he leave and let someone else do the dirty work? But he wanted so badly to see her and tell her about his cat. While he waited, Jovana and her boss showed up. They headed for the back door, but paused right outside and kissed first. It wasn't a short kiss, either, but an intimate one.

His instincts had been right all along. She'd been screwing her boss. So why did she always act like she wanted him, too? Unless she was one of those women who slept around. He cringed and shoved that thought from his mind as he watched the two of them separate and step inside.

Despite her unfaithful behavior, he would give her a chance as long as she apologized for what happened to his cat, Fred. And if she refused to give him what he wanted he'd take it anyway. That was the ultimate revenge. Better yet, he'd take it from her right in front of that idiot, Randy. A wicked grin tugged at his mouth and he stepped out of his car.

Another shot rang out and he ran to the door, now cracked open, hoping to protect her from whatever they'd stumbled upon so he could hurt her himself. He heard Jovana's hysterical crying and worried that she'd been shot. That would spoil all the fun. On light feet, he slipped inside and caught a glimpse of them dragging Jovana into the dining area. He searched for a kitchen knife, the bigger the better. From the sound of their voices the confrontation seemed to be taking place near the cash register.

He listened as one man cursed and said to the other, "Why'd you have to hit him so hard. What if you killed him? He's my boss."

"He's not gonna die. So what do we do with her now? She could testify against us."

"I don't know. Don't ask me."

Kurt slipped closer and peered into the other room.

The cook and his friend were standing by the register and the friend yelled, "Then I'll decide her fate. Now open it!" while holding Jovana flush against him.

"I don't know where the key is. Sometimes the boss takes it home with him."

The man with the tattoos pointed the gun at the other man's head and gestured toward the kitchen, where Randy lay sprawled on the kitchen floor next to Kurt. "Check him. Find that key."

"I don't see why this is necessary. I told you I'd pay you the rest if you gave me more time."

"Shut up, Shep! Stop acting like a wimp and just do it."

Jovana bit the man holding the gun. He swore and pushed her to the floor.

"Don't hurt her, man!"

"I'll do whatever I want. Now, what do we do with this little honey before her man wakes up?"

Randy groaned, but his eyes were still closed. Kurt looked down at him and saw his gun was still in the holster. Kurt grabbed it from Randy before he woke. He pressed his back against the door, his heart pounding as he peered around it to see where they stood. No one had noticed him yet.

Her assailant knelt in front of Jovana. She spat at him when he tried to kiss her, her face contorting like she couldn't contain her disgust. The man holding the gun now pointed it at Jovana and swore in her face, eliciting a squeal from her. Kurt stifled the urge to pounce on the jerk, but if he was going to make himself known, he had to be smart about it.

"Let her be. She's harmless," the man named Shep said.

The guy holding the gun now pointed it at Shep. "I said shut up! Now get me that key."

Kurt dodged his head behind the door again so the man heading toward him wouldn't see him. The moment Shep entered the kitchen and approached Randy, Kurt held the gun to the back of his head and whispered, "Say a word and I'll blow your head off."

The man raised his hands in the air and didn't put up a fight. He whispered back, "I'm innocent. He made me do this, I swear."

Kurt snorted. The man was a liar.

He glanced at Randy and back at Kurt as if wondering how they were connected.

The gunman in the other room grunted, unable to see him from where he stood, "What's taking so long?"

Kurt nodded for him to answer. "I looked but he doesn't have the key in his pocket."

The gunman swore again and shot his gun. That was three bullets now. Kurt heard a crashing sound amid Jovana's cries. Footsteps approached and the gunman entered the kitchen holding a half-blown apart register. "You're useless, you know tha--"

"Drop the gun." Tattoo man's eyes were so wide Kurt could see the whites all around. "I said drop the gun!"

He did as instructed, but then tossed the register toward Kurt, who saw it coming and pushed Shep in front of the flying object. It crashed into Shep's head and he hit the floor, falling on the other man's gun. Randy had yet to open his eyes.

As Tattoo Man tried to move him to get his gun, Kurt shot his hand. "Move again and I'll aim better next time."

The man screamed in pain and clutched his hand against his chest.

"Jovana, get the keys to the cooler and come in here. Now!"

She ran into the room and headed for the cooler. Grabbing the keys, she asked, "What you want me to do?"

Kurt nodded at the man with the bleeding hand. "You. Take your friend and drag him inside the cooler. If you don't put up a fight I may let you take your cash and run with it."

The bleeding man considered the offer for a moment and nodded. He hauled Shep up and the moment Kurt saw the other gun exposed he kicked it toward Jovana. "Grab the gun!"

She bent and quickly picked it up. Her hands shook, but she held it tight.

"Good. Now put him in the cooler."

The man obeyed.

"Grab the register and get out of here before I lose my patience with you and shoot you in a more delicate place."

The tattooed man grabbed the register with his good hand and took off running out the back door. He was loosing a lot of blood. The cops could easily find him in the ER if he didn't bleed to death first. Kurt smiled and praised himself for his own genius. He smiled at Jovana. "You can put the gun down now, honey."

She set the gun on the counter and nodded.

"Now lock the cooler so if he wakes up he can't get out."

Tears streamed down her face as she obeyed. The moment she locked the door, she turned and threw herself into Kurt's arms. "Thank you!"

Surprised by the turn of events and her sincere gratitude, he started to soften until he reminded himself of why he was there. He nudged her away from him and slipped the gun into the back of his belt. "I just came to tell you my cat died and I stumbled into this mess. Talk about good timing, eh?"

Jovana nodded and clung to him. "I am sorry about cat. Is my fault you gets flu."

So, even she recognized her own guilt. He hated that he was right. Now to claim her for himself. "Yes, it is. But I'll forgive you if give me some lovin', honey."

He offered her a seductive smile.

She glanced over at Randy, who lay on the floor. "I am sorry, but I cannot. I promise Randy I be his wife."

"What?" Kurt grabbed her shoulder. "How dare you betray me!"

"I did not betray! He ask me this. You did not ask."

"That's because you never called me back." He shoved her.

"I am... sorry... this is true." She stared at his hand and her eyes widened. "You hand is hurt. Did you... are you man who hits my door?"

"Yes, I wanted to talk to you about us. But it doesn't matter any more. I'm done with you. But first you're going to give me what I've been wanting. We're going to do it while he lays there and can hear us humping or I'll shoot him between the eyes and you'll do it anyway."

Jovana trembled violently, "No! I do anything you ask. Please do not hurt him."

"That's more like it baby." Kurt set the gun on the table and out of reach. "Now climb up on this counter here and take off your shirt. We'll start there."

Jovana nodded, tears streaming down her face, as she removed her shirt. She didn't even try to fight him. This was too easy. Part of him felt a twinge of guilt at pushing her to please him. He liked it much better when it was offered willingly. But she'd said she was going to marry Randy. Well so be it, but he was getting some first. Then he'd move on and find someone else. Arizona was starting to leave a bad taste in his mouth.

He tried to kiss her but she turned her face away. "Just use me and be done. I will not kiss you, but I will not fight you either."

Grabbing her shoulder, he squeezed hard and said, "I'll take what I want."

As he pressed his mouth on hers, she struggled against him.

He decided he liked it. Yeah, this way was definitely more exciting.

*****

Randy's head throbbed. He could hear Jovana's tearful pleas as she fought with someone, but he could barely move. How had his day taken on such a sick twist? He lay on the floor of his restaurant once again unable budge. Like before, he'd never seen the blow coming and the next thing he knew he was out cold.

He prayed like he'd never prayed before and tried to stand. He saw Jovana glance at him and continue arguing with Kurt. She was stalling for time. Good. He had to get up and help her. He patted his holster and found his gun missing. A quick search of the room revealed his gun on the counter a few feet away. The other was tucked in Kurt's pants, who removed it and set it on the counter behind him without looking back.

Randy only needed to reach one of them.

Jovana struggled on the counter as Kurt kissed her forcefully. He'd already removed her shirt and was now unzipping his pants. Blind fury filled Randy's veins as he stood, willing the white spots to clear as he moved his hand toward his 9MM. The moment his hand reached for the weapon, sirens whirred outside. Police cars were in the parking lot, lights now flashing. They must've approached quietly to surprise them so the criminals would be trapped.

Kurt swore and zipped his pants. He handed Jovana her shirt and yelled at her put it back on. "You will lie to them and say I saved you from these wicked men."

Jovana smiled as she pulled her shirt on and said, "Sorry I forget to say I call police when I was in other room. I knew they would catch you. You will not hurt me again."

Kurt turned and lunged for his weapon, but Randy stopped him.

A fight ensued and the other gun was knocked from the counter. Jovana ran for the back door and disappeared as Randy struggled with a man much stronger than he. But Kurt didn't use one of his hands, which gave Randy an advantage. He saw the scabs and swelling and knew that Kurt had been the jerk who had banged up the door.

He slammed Kurt's bad hand into the counter, then nailed him in the jaw with his elbow as he tried to keep him from reaching the guns. The police called through a bullhorn. "Come out with your hands up or we're coming after you."

Kurt ignored their threat and continued his attack. Randy took a punch to the eye that nearly knocked him on the floor. He heard commotion as he fought to stand and saw that several police officers had surrounded Kurt. Another officer pinned him to the floor and put cuffs on him.

"You're under arrest." Both men were read their Miranda rights. He was struggling to answer but the pain in his head and eye made it difficult.

145

Jovana started crying hysterically and ran to him. An officer tried to hold her back but she pushed past him and knelt next to Randy. "He is good man. He save me. Please do not do this."

Two officers spoke and one asked him. "You the manager? Do you have proof?"

"Yes, check my wallet. This is my restaurant and this man attacked my fiancé during the robbery. I was knocked out. When I came to I fought to keep him from grabbing one of those guns."

The other officer pulled out an evidence bag and picked up the guns with a gloved hand. He slipped them into their respective bags while the arresting officer unclipped the cuffs and released Randy. "I'll call an ambulance so they can look at your head."

Randy glanced over at Kurt and watched as one officer pulled his ID from his wallet. "Here's his wallet. He's not talking so look him up and let me know what you find."

"Yes, sir." The other officer went outside, probably to check their system for priors. Kurt frowned at Randy, but didn't speak. Two officers hauled him up to a standing position and guided him to the car.

Jovana went to the cooler and unlocked it. She wrapped some ice in a towel, then handed it to Randy. He placed it against the lump on his head and watched as Jovana showed the officer that there was another man on the floor in the cooler. He looked a lot like Shep. In broken English she tried to tell them he was one of the guys who robbed the restaurant. Randy watched and followed as she led the officer into the dining area. He saw the register was completely missing. So he had walked in on a robbery attempt. He hated that his instincts about Shep had been right all along.

An officer entered and told the man who appeared to be the lead officer. "Got a positive ID on him, sir. Kurt Smith is wanted in Pennsylvania for the murder of his wife. A warrant was just issued for his arrest last week. Looks like they were doing some construction where he buried the body in the woods near his house. They found it a few weeks ago when they were clearing the land for a housing project. Is this a stroke of luck, or what?"

Randy resisted the urge to vomit. While he hated to believe he was right about the man, at least Jovana would now be safe. But she'd come so close to disaster. He decided to not tell her what he knew about Kurt and let her find out later on the news when he could comfort her away from the crime scene. She couldn't handle any more bad stuff right now. He entered the dining area where an officer interviewed her. She smiled when she saw him and hugged him tight. "I love you, Ron-dee. You saves me."

While her comment made him smile, he realized her calling the police had been what actually made things turn in their favor. "You saved us by calling 9-1-1. That was very brave of you."

She smiled against his shirt. "You think this is true, but you still my hero."

Randy nodded at the officer, who smirked at her statement. No doubt he found it amusing.

"I'm done asking her questions. I need to interview you next. What's your name?"

As Randy held his precious woman, he answered all the questions he could. Relief flooded through him as he realized once again how close they'd come to disaster. He prayed silently, "Thank you, God, for delivering us from evil."

Several times in the middle of the interview he paused to kiss the top of Jovana's scalp because she refused to let go and trembled against him. He wanted to reassure her that she was safe now. When he finished answering the questions, he approached the window and pulled the blinds. No way was he opening *The Diner* today. He just wanted to take her home. Their customers could wait.

Chapter Twenty

Three and a half months later Randy glanced across the limo and admired his new bride. She had behaved so well since that terrifying incident at *The Diner*. Not once had she tried to kiss him or tempt him like she used to. He thanked God for their blossoming love and their holy union to come.

When he'd announced to Bojan and Laney that they were getting married, their enthusiastic support confirmed that he'd done the right thing by asking her to be his wife. He'd known God wanted him to marry her. But everyone's support made it that much firmer in his mind that he was completely in God's will by doing so.

She blushed and gave him a nervous smile in return. He'd learned a lot about her in the past three months. Like how she really didn't know what to do with a man who would not hurt her. They'd had a few spats along the way because of this, but once he realized she was just afraid that things would fall apart, he asked God to show him how to deal with her moods and reassure her of his love. God was faithful to answer and the healing in her life was now evident.

He winked at her, eliciting a few feminine giggles. She was so different from the seductive Jovana he'd struggled with months ago. They had agreed to refrain from kissing for the past three months to make their wedding night that much more exciting. Until the minister had told him he could kiss his bride, he'd behaved admirably. So when their lips finally met their kiss lasted much longer than what he'd observed at other weddings, drawing nervous laughter and applause from the wedding guests.

They'd breezed through the reception and now headed to their hotel room. Tonight they'd stay in Tucson, and in the morning they'd catch their flight to Macedonia. Jovana wanted all of her relatives to meet her new husband and he was more than willing to oblige. He wanted to know his wife better and observing her culture first hand, he believed, was the perfect place to start.

The limo pulled in front of a five star hotel. They entered the resort hand in hand and allowed the bellhop to carry their luggage to their room as they checked in. The heated glances Jovana sent his way made him anxious to get inside their suite and close the door.

He prayed she anticipated their uniting in the flesh with as much enthusiasm as he did. The look on her face made him think she looked forward to it. Several times over the past few months they'd had serious talks about his concerns regarding her experience and how much he lacked. When Jovana had reassured him that his love would please her and that no man had ever excited her with simple kisses before, his confidence grew and he no longer worried like he once had. He would love her like she'd never been loved before and it would all begin within the next few minutes.

They unlocked their suite and found a bottle of non-alcoholic champagne in a bucket of ice waiting for them. He cracked it open and poured them each a glass. The bellhop arrived with their luggage. He gave the young man a handsome tip and shooed him away. With a sly smile, he flicked the deadbolt shut and turned to beckon his new bride.

She brought him his glass of bubbly cider and they grinned at each other as they took little sips. He smiled wider, suddenly nervous now that they were alone.

Who would make the first move now that they could do whatever they wanted? Delicious shivers bolted through him as he set his glass down and tried to muster the courage to begin. Jovana did the same and she held his gaze. The questioning look in her eyes seemed to ask, "Can I?"

He offered her a slow, deliberate nod. He knew the moment she understood because she bolted into his arms and attacked him with such enthusiasm he hit the wall. This time he didn't stop her and carried her to their bed as she kissed his neck with enthusiasm.

As he laid her beneath him she stopped him with her hand and took a deep breath, her eyes filling with tears. "Ron-dee, you must know this. What I give tonight and for rest of my life is only for you. I have never loved man before like I love you."

He swallowed hard and blinked back tears of joy. His heart nearly burst at her sincerity. "Then you'll love me even if I'm not any good at this?"

Her delighted smile made him shiver. She unbuttoned the top button of his shirt and said, "We will learn together how to please each other."

"I like the sound of that." He tipped his head down to kiss her again, but she stopped him.

"Ron-dee, I... I am afraid."

That was the last thing he expected to hear. He hesitated and propped his head with his hand as he lay beside her, his eyes searching hers. "Why?"

"I do not know what to do." Tears filled her eyes and she looked helpless.

"You don't... That makes no sense." He hated thinking about her experience right now, but it was unavoidable after a comment like that.

"The feelings in my heart are so strong now they scare me. I do not know how to receive this love and my heart wants to run." She held his hands. "I will trust, but you must know this frighten me."

"Then I'll be gentle. You let me do all the work. Relax and receive what I offer."

"I do nothing?" Her puzzled expression made him smile. Poor girl really was confused.

"Just receive my love, Jovana. It's all I have to offer besides my heart."

A tender smile formed on her face and she touched his whiskered chin with her finger, tracing it. "Okay, I will give you this gift. I will receive your love."

He waited a moment, then kissed her slowly, but with restrained passion. He sensed her fear melting and his heart pounded with anticipation as she received his affection. He had waited his entire life for this moment and he wasn't messing it up.

She chuckled as he kissed her again, making him pull back.

"You right. This very nice, and is easy."

A deep chuckle escaped him and he kissed the tip of her nose, his desire building from the wait. "Good, my lovely wife. Cause I'm about to make it harder on you."

She squealed as he tackled her with kisses. Something told him marriage to this amazing woman would never be boring. As she wriggled beneath him and giggled, he laughed.

The joy they now shared made his heart sing. She responded like an innocent young woman who hadn't been destroyed by a sick man's twisted passions. He thanked the Lord for the miracle that had taken place in her life and how her new last name now fit her brave spirit.

Jovana Strong was his best friend, his confidant, and finally, thank God, his wife.

The End

About Michelle Sutton

Michelle Sutton has been reading since she was in kindergarten but never enjoyed writing, and she certainly never expected to be an author herself. However, in 2003, she felt God calling her to write. Once she got started she discovered she has no desire to stop. Now she is a multi-published, award-winning author of numerous romantic fiction titles. She still reads a lot of books and in her spare time writes reviews for a variety of blogs and websites as a media reviewer. Michelle lives with her husband and two sons on a four-acre ranch in sunny Arizona.

Read more about Michelle at: http://www.MichelleSutton.net